STAR WARS
THE RISE AND FALL OF
DARTH VADER

BY RYDER WINDHAM

SCHOLASTIC INC.

New York   Toronto   London   Auckland   Sydney   Mexico City   New Delhi   Hong Kong   Buenos Aires

No part of this publication may be reproduced, stored in a retrieval system, or transmitted in any form or by any means, electronic, mechanical, photocopying, recording, or otherwise, without written permission of the publisher. For information regarding permission, write to Scholastic Inc., Attention: Permissions Department, 557 Broadway, New York, NY 10012.

ISBN-13: 978-0-439-68133-9
ISBN-10: 0-439-68133-2

Cover art by Drew Struzan

Design by Phil Falco

12 11 10 9 8 7 6 5 4 3   10 11 12 13 14/0

Printed in the U.S.A.

First printing, April 2009

For Ralph McQuarrie

ACKNOWLEDGMENTS

Sincere thanks to the screenwriters of the *Star Wars* films: George Lucas, Lawrence Kasdan, Leigh Brackett, and Jonathan Hales. I am also in debt to Terry Brooks, James Luceno, Kilian Plunkett, Daniel Wallace, and the late Brian Daley and Archie Goodwin, whose respective *Star Wars* books, comics, and radio dramatizations provided material for various sequences in this novel. Special thanks to Dorothy Windham for research assistance, to Violet Windham for never letting me win a lightsaber fight, to Anne Windham for helping me in every way to make time to complete this book, and to *Star Wars* fans Titus DosRemedios and Peter Ricci for sharing their ideas and concerns about Darth Vader. As ever, big thanks to David Levithan at Scholastic, and to Jonathan Rinzler and Leland Chee at Lucasfilm.

STAR·WARS

THE RISE AND FALL OF

DARTH VADER

PROLOGUE

Darth Vader, the Dark Lord of the Sith, was dreaming.

In his dream, he saw his own dark form standing upon the open terrace that clung to the curved outer wall of Bast Castle, his private fortress on the planet Vjun. Freezing acidic rain pelted his helmet, and high winds tore at his black cloak with incredible fury, as if the weather itself was doing its best to kill him along with anything else that attempted to live on the barren world. And yet Vader felt more alive than he had in years.

Turning from the balcony, he entered a vaulted doorway, leaving a trail of wet bootprints on the corridor floor. The walls were lined with automated heating vents that dried his garments as he strode to the dimly illuminated observatory. Although few had ever treaded within his fortress, he was not surprised to find the young man who stood at the center of the domed-ceiling chamber.

1

The young man was Luke Skywalker.

Clad in form-fitting black clothes, Luke had his back to Vader as he examined a three-dimensional star map that was suspended in the air above a holoprojector. Vader recognized the map as the Coruscant Sector. Luke's arms hung at his sides, and Vader noticed that Luke's right hand, clad in a black glove, was almost touching the light-saber clipped to his belt.

A new lightsaber, Vader thought. *And a new hand.*

Silent as a shadow, Vader moved forward into the room.

Without acknowledging Vader, Luke raised his right arm into the holographic starfield. He moved his cybernetic fingers through the tiny, glittering orb that represented the planet Coruscant.

"The Emperor is dead," Luke said in a low voice. "All that was his is now yours."

"No, my son," Vader said. "The galaxy is *ours*."

Luke nodded and smiled. Vader was still facing Luke when a low, familiar voice muttered unexpectedly from behind, "You are both . . . wrong."

It was the voice of Emperor Palpatine. Vader saw Luke's expression become tense, but he did not turn to face the Emperor. Then the Emperor began to laugh.

A ring of fire erupted from the floor, surrounding Vader and cutting him off from Luke. Listening to his Master's cackle, Vader lowered his masked head and thought, *Why won't you die?*

The laughter continued. Luke said, "He *can't* be alive! Father, help me!"

Around Vader, the fire began to burn inward, moving closer toward his body. Behind his helmet, Vader tried to blot out the horrid laughter. *Why won't you ever die?*

But the laughter did not stop. Vader attempted to reach for his own lightsaber, but his arm suddenly felt like it was made of solid stone. The flames were now licking at his cloak and boots. The Emperor laughed louder. Luke began to scream.

Vader squeezed his eyes shut. He could smell fused circuits and roasting flesh.

WHY WON'T YOU EVER —?!

And then Vader awoke.

Darth Vader's eyes snapped open. Seated within his pressurized meditation chamber aboard his personal Super Star Destroyer, the *Executor*, his first waking thought was, *Jedi don't have nightmares.* This thought surprised him almost as much as the intensity of the imagery of Bast Castle. It had been over two decades since he had broken from the Jedi order to become a Sith Lord, and in all those years, he had not thought about whether Jedi had nightmares, or dreams for that matter. Not since the end of the Clone Wars.

Perhaps it was a premonition, Vader thought, as a vein pulsed against the left temple of his bare, horribly scarred head. He quickly rejected this notion. He knew a premonition when he had one, knew that it was more than just a trick of the imagination mixing with subconscious desires. The vision of his fortress had been something else.

Perhaps a warning, but from whom? Vader considered the possibility that the vision had been planted in his mind by a skilled telepath. The idea that he might have been violated made him angry, and his anger opened him to the dark side of the Force. Closing his eyes, he reached out with the Force and searched for signs of psychic energy trails that might lead to a telepathic invader. He found nothing, no one. . . .

But the Emperor would not leave a trail.

Vader grimaced. A year had passed since his last encounter with Luke Skywalker on Cloud City, where he had revealed his identity to Luke and told him it was his destiny to destroy the Emperor. Vader suspected that the Emperor knew of this treachery, for the Emperor knew everything eventually. But even if the Emperor were aware of all that had transpired, Vader was certain he would not feel threatened. The Emperor was simply too powerful. And yet somehow, Vader sensed that the Emperor had nothing to do with his strange vision of Bast Castle.

Could it have been just a dream? Vader wasn't sure. After so many years without dreaming, he had forgotten what dreams were like.

Above his pale head, a retractable robotic arm held

his helmet close against the spherical chamber's ceiling. Dedicated servos lowered the helmet over his head and locked it onto his collar's hermetic seal. As his damaged lungs exhaled through his armored suit's life-support system, a deep hiss was emitted from his triangular respiratory vent.

The upper half of the meditation chamber lifted, exposing Vader like a black pistil at the center of a white mechanical flower. His seat rotated, allowing him to face a wide viewscreen, which flicked on to display the image of Admiral Piett on the *Executor*'s bridge.

Vader said, "Status report."

"The *Executor* is prepared to leave Coruscant's orbit," Piett replied, standing at attention in his gray uniform. Although his voice was alert, his eyes appeared tired from staring at sensor screens and navigational monitors. "I await your command."

"Set course for the Endor system," Vader said.

"As you wish, my lord." Piett's image vanished from the viewscreen.

It was definitely not a dream, Vader convinced himself without difficulty. *Dreams are for pathetic life-forms.* He stared at his own reflection on the surface of the viewscreen.

I am the nightmare.

With an imperceptible gesture, he reset the viewscreen to display the starfield that lay directly before the *Executor*'s bow. As he gazed at the distant stars on the screen, a deeply buried memory pushed its way into his consciousness. It was the memory of a wish, a wish to visit every star in the galaxy. But that wish, and the dreams that went with it, had belonged to someone else, a child who lived a long time ago and was no more.

Those were the dreams of a boy named Anakin Skywalker.

CHAPTER ONE

Anakin Skywalker was dreaming.

In the dream, he was an older boy, but still years away from manhood. He was inside the open cockpit of a small repulsorlift vehicle, soaring over rocky terrain at an incredibly high speed. Two strong cables were secured to a parallel pair of long engines in front of the vehicle, and the gap between the engines was bridged by an arc of crackling energy. Anakin had never seen such a strange contraption, but somehow he knew how to handle it. As he pressed against a throttle lever and plunged into a high-walled ravine, he realized, *I'm a pilot!*

He wasn't alone. Several similar vehicles swerved through the ravine in front of him, and the noise of their engines, echoing off the rocky walls, was almost deafening.

It's a race!

With fearless precision, Anakin accelerated and whipped past the other vehicles. Out of the corners of his eyes, he caught fleeting glimpses of his competition. Most were aliens he'd never seen before, but they all had alert, determined expressions and nimble fingers. Anakin had dreamed of other worlds before, but never anyplace like this.

Launching out of the ravine, Anakin led the other racers across a wide expanse of desert flats. Twin suns blazed in the sky, baking the hard sand so that the rising heat shimmered in the air and made distant rock formations appear to float above the planetary surface. In the distance, he sighted an enormous, open arena that was ringed by crowded grandstands and dome-topped towers. He knew the finish line was in that arena. Tightening his grip on the controls, he thought, *I'm going to win!*

Suddenly, his left engine began to shudder, violently jolting the cable that linked the engine to his vehicle. Anakin was struggling to maintain control when his right engine let out a loud whine, then both engines began to nose toward the ground. Anakin squirmed in his cockpit and cried, *"NO!"*

"It's all right, Ani," said his mother's voice.

And then Anakin Skywalker woke up.

The shuddering sensation and loud whine of an engine continued as Anakin opened his eyes. He was huddled beside his mother on a hard metal bench in a space freighter's cargo compartment, which was separated from the noisy engine room by a crisscross of metal bars. The cargo hold was tightly packed with thirty other beings, aliens as well as humans; those who didn't have a seat on one of the four long benches either stood or crouched on the filthy floor.

Anakin looked up to his mother's pale, grime-covered face and said, "We're landing?"

"It feels like we are," Shmi Skywalker answered with a smile. She gently pushed Anakin's blond hair back from his forehead and gazed into his blue eyes. "You had a bad dream?"

Anakin thought for a moment, then said, "Not too bad." He wished the cargo hold had some kind of a window, or even a small viewscreen so he could see what was going on outside. "Know where we're going yet?"

"Not yet."

Before they had boarded the freighter, a crewman had explained that only paying passengers were allowed to know their destination in advance, and all others — for security reasons — would just have to wait. Shmi had hoped to make Anakin feel better about the situation by reminding him that she always liked surprises, but he sensed she was scared. She took his little hand in hers and said, "Just hold tight."

When the freighter stopped shaking and the engine's whine began to die, the cargo hold's occupants shifted out of their seats and up from the floor. Standing beside his mother while she strapped the ragged bag that contained their few belongings to her back, Anakin wished he were taller so he wouldn't feel so crushed between all the adult bodies. He also wished for some fresh air, as the hold's single refresher had backed up and everyone, including himself, smelled awful. They'd been waiting for several minutes for the exit hatch to open when Shmi looked down at Anakin and said, "Do you want me to carry you?"

Anakin's legs weren't tired, but he nodded.

Moving carefully to avoid bumping the surrounding people, Shmi lifted her son and held him close against her chest. As he wrapped his small arms around her neck, he said, "Thanks."

"You're getting big," she told him. "It won't be long before you'll be carrying me."

"Really?"

Shmi laughed. "Don't worry, you're not growing *that* fast."

An older woman standing behind Shmi smiled at Anakin and asked, "How old are you?"

Anakin smiled back and held up three fingers. In fact, he wasn't certain that he was three years old, but he didn't want to admit that he didn't know.

The hatch finally opened and the compartment was instantly flooded by a blast of hot, dry air. Even those who had been eager to leave the cramped cargo hold were suddenly reluctant to walk down the ramp that led outside. The heat reminded Anakin of his dream. Moving his lips close to his mother's ear, he whispered, "Twin suns."

Before Shmi could ask what he was talking about, a voice from below shouted, "Come on, move it out!"

The people filed out of the freighter. They found themselves on a sandy stretch of land near a cluster of domed, low-level adobe structures. Air traffic indicated they had landed at the outskirts of a fairly busy spaceport. A few pedestrians were visible in the distance, moving slowly and keeping to the shade of the windowless buildings in an effort to avoid the blistering heat.

"Welcome back to Mos Espa, O mighty Gardulla," a voice bellowed in thick Huttese. Anakin, still carried by his mother, turned his head to see the speaker was a green-skinned male Rodian who stood at the bottom of the ramp that extended from the freighter's main hatch. While the Rodian made a sweeping bow, Gardulla the Hutt, the massive sluglike alien who had chartered the freighter, descended on a repulsorsled that glided down the ramp from the freighter's main hatch. Gardulla immediately began issuing orders to her attendants. Anakin knew enough Huttese to comprehend that Gardulla was eager to see something called a Podrace.

Shmi set Anakin down on the ground. He squinted up at the sky and said, "See, Mom? Told you."

Shmi followed his gaze to the two suns overhead, and then she understood what he'd said moments earlier. "*Twin suns.* Yes, I see."

Anakin wanted to tell his mother about the dream he'd had, but they had to remain quiet as one of

Gardulla's attendants, a long-necked Anx, began to bark out instructions. The Anx pointed to Anakin, Shmi, and six other people, and said, "You'll be sharing living quarters at Gardulla's estate, here in Mos Epsa. Before you're escorted there, be aware your implanted transmitters have been set for —"

Anakin was wondering if *living quarters* meant more than one room when the Anx was interrupted by the loud report of a blaster pistol that sounded like it came from the nearby adobe buildings. At the sound of the shot, Anakin stood still while everyone else near the freighter flinched, ducked, or dived for cover behind the few cargo containers that had already been removed from the ship. Shmi threw her body protectively in front of her son, but he pushed his arms out, pressing away from her so he could see what was happening.

A reptilian humanoid bolted out from an alley between two adobe buildings and ran toward the freighter. As it drew closer, Anakin saw the runner was a lean Arcona with an anvil-shaped head and clear, marblelike eyes. A metal fetter with a long, broken chain was secured to the Arcona's right ankle, making a jangling sound as it whipped behind his running feet. A moment later, two blaster-wielding men jumped from the alley, and Anakin realized the Arcona was running for his life.

Seeing the men with blasters about to shoot in the direction of the freighter, Gardulla's Anx attendant bellowed in Huttese, "Hold your fire, you fools!" Then he pointed a long, pointed finger at the fleeing Arcona and yelled to Gardulla's guards, "Stop him!"

The guards spread out quickly. Without breaking his pace, the Arcona elbowed a guard aside and dodged another. Anakin could see that the Arcona was trying to get away from his pursuers, but he had no idea where the Arcona was trying to go. Except for some low dunes, the surrounding land was almost entirely flat, with no other ships or vehicles in sight. *Nowhere to hide,* Anakin thought.

The Arcona's frightened eyes flicked toward Anakin, and the boy held his gaze. Anakin felt sorry for the Arcona and wished he could help. Then one of Gardulla's guards lunged forward and the Arcona sprinted away, moving past Anakin and the others. He was about two meters away from Anakin when his body erupted in a small explosion.

Anakin blinked as the Arcona's remains fell to the ground. He turned quickly to look at the two men who had chased the Arcona away from the buildings. Neither man had fired a blaster. Anakin was observant enough to realize that the Arcona had not been shot, and that some explosive device had detonated within him.

Shmi pulled Anakin close to her side and said, "Look away, Ani."

Anakin ignored her and kept his eyes on what was left of the Arcona. A few of the guards and the Anx attendant walked over to inspect the smoldering mess.

Noticing Anakin, the Anx turned his long, pointed chin to the boy and said, "That's what happens to slaves who try to escape on Tatooine."

Anakin felt his throat become painfully dry. No matter how often his mother reminded him that there were less fortunate beings in the galaxy, there was no denying the fact that they were both slaves, the property of Gardulla the Hutt.

Tatooine, thought Anakin. *Welcome to Tatooine.*

CHAPTER TWO

Slavery was illegal throughout Republic space, but the planet Tatooine was in the galaxy's Outer Rim Territories, where the laws of the Republic rarely applied.

Shmi Skywalker had been a slave almost her entire life, ever since space pirates captured her family during a space voyage. Separated from her parents at a young age, she had changed owners many times. One former master, Pi-Lippa, had been kind and had taught Shmi valuable technical skills. Though Pi-Lippa had planned to free Shmi, she'd died before she could, and Shmi instead became the property of one of Pi-Lippa's relatives, who did not want to free her.

Before coming into Gardulla's ownership, Shmi had given birth to Anakin. Shmi could not explain Anakin's conception — there had been no father — but she accepted him as the greatest gift she could have ever received.

In the months that followed his arrival on Tatooine, Anakin kept his eyes and ears open. He eavesdropped on conversations between Gardulla's attendants, guards, and other slaves, and watched carefully when mechanics and technicians came to repair or replace sand-fouled machinery. He wanted to learn everything he could about the desert world, its inhabitants, and their technologies, because he believed such knowledge might be the only way he and his mother would ever find freedom.

And so he learned about the early colonists of Tatooine, the miners whose search for valuable minerals ended as an astronomically expensive disappointment. Some of the miners chose to remain on the desert world while others were simply stranded. One of the first human settlements was at a place called Fort Tusken, which was assaulted by Tatooine's indigenous humanoids, the nomadic Sand People, who subsequently became known as Tusken Raiders. Favoring traditional club and ax weapons, Sand People wore head-concealing sandproof masks, and heavy cloaks that protected them from the elements and helped them blend in with the landscape. Sand People never adapted to easy contact with settlers, and were reputed to be as ferocious as they were mysterious. Anakin had yet to see them, but had been told that it was their howls he sometimes heard after darkness fell. He found them bloodcurdling.

Tatooine's other significant natives were the Jawas, diminutive beings with glowing eyes who salvaged the miners' enormous abandoned vehicles to scavenge the desert for any scrap of metal or bit of junk that they could transform into goods for sale or trade. Although Jawas were almost as malodorous as a backed-up refresher, Anakin looked forward to their visits to Gardulla's estate because he learned a great deal by watching them work. Much to the amazement of the other slaves and a few attendants, Anakin quickly gained a reputation for being able to fix discarded appliances.

As for Gardulla, Anakin learned that she competed with an even larger Hutt, named Jabba, over control of various enterprises on Tatooine. Anakin also discovered that Gardulla fed those who displeased her to a monstrous krayt dragon that she kept in a pit beneath her fortresslike palace off Mos Espa Way, and that she was addicted to betting on the Podraces. Anakin was in no hurry to meet any krayt dragons, but he was intrigued by everything he heard about the dangerous, high-speed sport that involved a pair of repulsorlift engines tethered to an open-cockpit vehicle. The first time he overheard two of Gardulla's attendants discussing the design of a Podracer they'd seen, he remembered the dream he'd had just before he arrived on Tatooine. According to the attendants, Podracing was the biggest attraction in Mos Espa, and it drew crowds from all over the galaxy. Anakin wondered if he'd ever get to watch a Podrace.

A few months after his arrival to Mos Espa, Anakin was helping a late-model droid mechanic repair a portable vaporator near the estate's main entrance when a winged, pudgy-bellied Toydarian with a flexible trunklike nose flew into the courtyard. Seeing the boy, the Toydarian paused, hovering in the air, and examined Anakin's handiwork. Speaking in Huttese, the Toydarian said in a low, wheezy voice, "You put in that water pump unit the wrong way."

Anakin had been told not to talk with strangers, but he cautiously replied, "I rigged it." Seeing that the Toydarian seemed genuinely interested, he demonstrated the pump mechanism and added, "I made it work better."

The Toydarian's eyes went wide as he watched the pump in fluid operation. "Hmm . . . who showed you how to rig it?"

"Nobody," Anakin said. His mother had told him not to brag, but he could not help feeling proud. "I just . . . I figured it out. My mom can fix things too."

"Is that so?" The Toydarian lowered himself in the air to examine the unit more closely. "You're not bad with your hands, kid," he said. "Not bad at all."

Anakin bowed his head slightly and said, "Thank you, sir."

"I have an appointment with Gardulla," the Toydarian said. Then he winked and rubbed his clawed fingers together and added, "A matter of money!"

Anakin didn't know how to respond to that, but just then, Gardulla herself heaved her bulky body into the entrance and said, "Ready to pay up, Watto?"

"Maybe, maybe," the Toydarian said as he hovered toward Gardulla. "But the next race is tomorrow, and I have an idea for another bet. . . ."

Anakin watched the Toydarian follow Gardulla into the main building, then went back to work on the vaporator.

Gardulla lost her bet with Watto.

Two days later, Anakin and Shmi had a new owner.

When Watto wasn't gambling, he ran one of the most successful parts dealerships in Mos Epsa. He had need for someone with Anakin's mechanical aptitude, and had plenty of work for Shmi, too. Both mother and son were grateful to Watto for keeping them together, and after sharing a dingy, fetid room with six other slaves at Gardulla's estate, they were astonished to learn they would have an entire hovel to themselves at Slave Quarters Row, along the outskirts of Mos Espa. Watto believed they *should* feel grateful, and made it clear that if they didn't do as he said, he'd fill the hovel to capacity with additional slaves.

As days turned into weeks and months became years, Anakin made the best of his time, learning all that he could about technology and interstellar travel. He studied the aliens who passed through Mos Espa and got to know the local merchants on a first-name basis. While sitting in junked starship cockpits, he learned to recognize the controls for thrusters, stabilizers, and repulsors. From watching other mechanics and pit droids, he became proficient at repairing Podracers at Watto's shop.

By age seven, he began to secretly salvage bits and pieces to restore a junked Podracer cockpit and a pair of Radon-Ulzer 620C engines that he hoped to transform into his very own Podracer. He kept this project under the cover of an old tarp in an area of the common refuse dump in back of the slave housing, where Watto never ventured, and deliberately kept the Podracer looking like it would never run. If Watto ever found out about it, he would dismiss it as just some childish project.

Watto *did* catch Anakin taking a refurbished Podracer for a test spin around the junkyard, but the Toydarian's fury died when he realized how well the boy handled the vehicle. Like Gardulla, Watto was addicted to gambling on Podraces, and he could hardly believe his good fortune, to own a slave who might generate revenue at the racetrack. Despite Anakin's age and species, he was tested and soon qualified to become a Podrace pilot. Much to his mother's horror, he eventually began competing under Watto's sponsorship.

Watto never stopped threatening to buy more slaves, but Anakin and his mother continued to have the hovel for themselves. Watto even gave Shmi an aeromagnifier that she could use to clean computer memory devices, allowing her to bring in a modest income. Despite these advantages, Anakin did not give up on his dreams of freedom. He began thinking of making some kind of a scanner to locate the transmitter implanted in his body, even though he wasn't sure how such a transmitter might be deactivated or removed.

At some point, while listening to spacers talk of far-away worlds, he became aware of the Jedi Knights, the powerful peacekeepers of the Galactic Republic, who used lightsabers: a handheld weapon that emitted a lethal, truncated laser beam. Despite his limited knowledge of the Jedi, he sometimes had dreams of becoming one. Anakin wondered if any Jedi had ever heard of Tatooine, or if any had been born into slavery.

By age nine, he was resigned to the fact that he wasn't leaving Tatooine any time soon.

Still, every night, lying in the darkness of his small room that was cluttered with his various homemade devices and scientific projects, he vowed: *I won't be a slave forever.*

CHAPTER THREE

"How's your Podracer coming along, Ani?" his friend Kitster asked as he stepped over a rusted landspeeder turbine in Watto's junkyard.

Anakin shot a startled look at the dark-haired boy. "Keep your voice down!" Anakin said in a low voice. "You want Watto to find out?"

Kitster lowered his own voice and said, "Sorry, I forgot. How long have you been working on it?"

"Almost two years," Anakin admitted as he picked up a worn gasket.

"You really think it'll fly?"

"Once I get a few more parts, sure it will," Anakin said, tossing the gasket aside. "Problem is, if I fly it, Watto will know I *have* it, and then he'll want to take it from me. I'll just have to keep it a secret, and keep flying *his* cruddy Pods."

"I'd like to try flying a Podracer someday," Kitster said wistfully.

"Maybe you will." Anakin didn't want to hurt Kitster's feelings, but he knew that his friend wouldn't last five seconds in a Podrace. Operating a Podracer required incredibly fast reflexes, the competition was fierce, and Anakin — as far as anyone knew — was the only human ever to fly one and live. Despite this accomplishment, Anakin knew he'd have to do better to please Watto. In the more than half-dozen races he had competed in so far, he had crashed twice and failed to finish even once. The biggest challenge he had was dealing with Sebulba, the gangly, crook-legged, antagonistic Dug, who won often and cheated almost constantly. Sebulba never hesitated to force competitors off the course, and had caused more than a dozen pilots to crash in the past year alone. Anakin thought, *If it weren't for that cheat, I'd have won by now!*

Kitster asked, "Think you'll win the next race?"

Anakin shrugged. "I'd be happy just to make it to the finish."

Anakin turned to another pile of metal, and found himself looking at a pair of slotted lenses that were surrounded by multicolored wires contained within a skull-shaped metal armature. Strangely, the lenses seemed to be staring back at him, and he realized they were burned-out photoreceptors. "Hey, Kitster!" he said as he picked up the object. "Look what I found!"

"What is it?"

"A droid head!" Anakin said, brushing sand from

the vocoder plate beneath the photoreceptors, which had served as the droid's eyes. "And not a pit droid's either!" The head's metal plating had been removed, and the exposed photoreceptors had a surprised, wide-eyed expression. He handed the head to Kitster.

"It's pretty beat up," Kitster observed. "Maybe it was some kind of war droid?"

"I don't think so," Anakin said as he looked around, hoping to find some other droid parts. "The metal's pretty thin — Oh, WOW!" His gaze had fallen on what appeared to be the decapitated head's skeletal body, which lay in a tangled heap beside a pile of discharged fuel cells. Like the head, the body was without plating, but Anakin was delighted just the same. "The whole structural framework's there! You know what this *means*, don't you?"

Kitster thought hard. "Umm, no."

"It means I can build my own —"

"Boy!" Watto's voice interrupted, calling from beyond the arched portal that separated the junkyard from his bell-shaped shop. "Boy! Where in this dump are you?!"

"Oh, no!" Anakin said, glancing at Kitster and then back to the archway. "Wait here!" Trying hard to maintain a relaxed expression, he trotted out of the junkyard.

"Ah! There you are!" Watto said when he sighted Anakin. Hovering outside the entrance of his shop, he spoke in Huttese, "For a moment, I suspected you'd run away from Watto."

"Oh, and give you the pleasure of seeing my transmitter detonate?"

"Pleasure?" Watto said, his trunklike nose turning slightly upward as if recoiling from Anakin's words. "You think I like cleaning up exploded slaves? Bweh heh heh!" When he was done laughing, he gestured with a three-fingered hand to some more scrap-filled containers that had just been delivered, and said, "Now get back to work! I want this scrap sorted by noon!"

After Anakin had hauled the containers into the junkyard, he returned to where he'd left Kitster with the droid parts.

"You're not telling Watto about the droid?" Kitster asked.

"I found him. He's mine," Anakin said as he began dragging the droid's body into an area shaded by large metal refuse, where Watto was unlikely to notice it. "Besides, Watto wouldn't be able to fix him. I'll smuggle him back home, piece by piece."

Handing the droid's head to Anakin, Kitster said, "But even if you get him to work, what'll you use him for?"

"Lots of things. Running errands. Lifting stuff. . . . Hey, what's this?" He had found a line of small engraved lettering at the base of the droid's skull, and he held the head out so Kitster could see it too. "Says here he's a *Cybot Galactica Protocol Droid*."

"Protocol? What's that good for?"

"I don't know," Anakin admitted. "I'll have to ask my mom. Hey, maybe he'll even help me and my mom leave Tatooine!" Holding the droid's head in both hands, Anakin studied its mechanisms more closely. "The balance gyro's ancient. I'm guessing seventy or eighty years old. I'll bet he saw a lot of action. Makes you wonder . . . how did he wind up like this?"

Anakin gazed into the droid's burnt-out eyes as if he might find more clues to the droid's history there. But he saw only the droid's frozen, startled expression. *Don't worry, pal*, Anakin thought. *I'll take good care of you.*

It took five days of stealthy maneuvers for Anakin to move the droid's remains from the junkyard to his hovel. Except for Kitster, he told no one about the droid. But he should have told at least one other person: his mother, who was *not* happy to enter the hovel and find her son's latest project laid out in hundreds of dirty pieces on the dining table.

Shmi had bought a small sack of dried vegetables at the market, and she placed them on the kitchen counter. Not wanting to look at the bizarre metal and wire skeleton that lay in a supine position on the table with its dead eyes staring at the ceiling, she averted her gaze from Anakin and the droid. "Let me guess," she said. "You *found* it?"

"Yeah, pretty lucky, huh? And . . . well, I don't know anyone else in Mos Espa who'd be able to fix him up right. If I hadn't saved him from the scrap heap, he might have wound up smelted!" When Shmi didn't respond, Anakin felt compelled to add, "He's a *protocol* droid, Mom. Do you know what that is?"

Shmi took a deep breath and turned around to face Anakin. "Protocol droids speak millions of languages. They're used as translators. By diplomats."

"Oh," Anakin said. He could tell by the tone of his mother's voice that she thought they would have no use for a protocol droid. Hoping to convince her otherwise, he continued, "Oh! That's . . . that's great! He'll be *really* useful at the market if we want to trade with a merchant who doesn't speak Basic. And . . . and just imagine how impressed visitors will be when he greets them at the door! I'm sure he'll be good at helping us in lots of other ways too."

Shmi returned her attention to the vegetables.

"He'll need new photoreceptors," Anakin said. "I think I can find some at Watto's shop."

"You're being careless, Ani," Shmi said with concern. "Watto will be enraged if he learns you've taken an entire droid."

"But I *had* to do it, Mom! The moment I saw all the parts were there, I just knew I had to put him back together." Anakin gently gripped the droid's right forearm and lifted it up from the table, testing the flexibility

27

of the elbow joint. "Looking at him, all torn up and busted . . . it just made me so sad. If protocol droids are good with languages and translating, I'll bet he was really smart." Anakin looked at the droid's face again. "I'd also bet he didn't have a friend in the galaxy. Why else would he end up in a scrap heap on Tatooine?"

"Maybe it talked too much," Shmi said.

"Aw, Mom. You'll hurt his feelings."

"The droid is a machine, Ani. It doesn't have feelings."

"How do you know?" Anakin said, unable to keep the hurt from his voice. "Maybe his owners were mean to him and didn't care what happened to him. Maybe he tried to escape. Maybe . . . he was just like us."

Shmi felt Anakin's sorrow, and thought of the slave that had died while trying to escape five days earlier. She turned to her son, put her hands on his shoulders, and said, "Promise me, Ani. When you . . . *find* a new pair of photoreceptors for our new friend . . . you won't get caught."

"You mean, I can keep him?"

Shmi nodded as she surveyed the droid. "It's clear to me now. You were meant to help this droid. You're his second chance."

"Thanks, Mom!" Anakin said as he hugged his mother. "When I get him to talk, I'll tell him to thank you too!"

"No, Ani. After all, *you'll* be his maker. Just remember, the droid is your responsibility. And unless you're prepared to care for something, you don't deserve to have it."

"I won't forget," Anakin said.

"And one more thing," Shmi added in a severe tone.

"Yes, Mom?"

"I want the droid off our dining table right *now*."

CHAPTER FOUR

The next race did not go well for Anakin. Flying a Podracer owned by Watto, he was neck-and-neck with Sebulba — when the cheating Dug flashed his Pod's thrusters at Anakin's cockpit, nearly smashing him into the area of the racecourse known as Metta Drop. Anakin survived, but he crashed Watto's Pod, damaging both engines. Watto was furious, and Shmi made it clear to Anakin that she didn't want him to race anymore, even if Watto decided he wanted Anakin to compete again.

A little more than a week after the crash, Anakin had his protocol droid's intelligence and communications processors up and running. Although the droid had no memory of how he arrived on Tatooine, he counted Jawa and Tusken among the six million languages he spoke. The droid uttered clipped sentences in a well-mannered voice, but for some reason didn't always know when to *stop* talking. He also worried a lot. Anakin named the droid C-3PO, choosing the number three because he considered the droid the third member of his family after his mother and himself. C-3PO was still without metal coverings and had only a single working eye, but when Watto instructed Anakin to take a speeder loaded with scrap metal and other goods to the Dune Sea to do some trading with the Jawas, Anakin decided to secretly bring the droid along for the four-standard-hours round-trip.

Anakin and C-3PO met the Jawas in the shadow of the sandcrawler beside Mochot Steep, a singular rock formation about halfway across the Dune Sea. C-3PO proved to be a capable translator by helping Anakin negotiate with the Jawas, who were sometimes known to barter damaged goods. When the trading was done, Anakin had acquired two mechanic droids, three serviceable multipurpose droids, and a damaged hyperdrive converter that needed only minor repairs.

Heading back to Mos Espa, Anakin was guiding the droid-loaded speeder through the Xelric Draw, a shallow, widemouthed canyon near the edge of the Dune Sea, when he sighted something. It was a shadowy shape that seemed out of place at the base of the rocky canyon's walls. As Anakin veered toward the area that had attracted his attention, C-3PO became nervous and fixed his one working eye on his maker.

"Master Anakin, whatever are you doing?" C-3PO said with concern. "Mos Espa is down the canyon draw, not through the side of the — oh, my! Is that what I think it is?" C-3PO had sighted the shape too, and because he'd learned about the more dangerous life-forms on Tatooine, he didn't like what he saw. "Master, there is every reason to turn right around —"

"I know," Anakin interrupted. "I just want a look."

Anakin brought the speeder to a stop near the cliff wall. A pile of rocks rested below the wall, and under the rocks lay a motionless, humanoid body, with one leg pinned beneath a large boulder. The body wore a tan robe, leather gloves, and boots. It was sprawled face-down, head turned to one side, allowing Anakin to see the cloth-wrapped head, its face concealed by goggles and a breath mask. A long, dual-handled blaster rifle lay about a meter away from one oustretched arm.

Anakin had heard enough about Tusken Raiders to know what they looked like. But he'd never seen one up close before.

From the speeder, Anakin surveyed the cliff wall's gouged, broken surface. He easily imagined that the Tusken had been hiding somewhere above when the rocks that had supported him gave way, sending him crashing to the canyon floor. Anakin climbed out of the speeder for a closer look.

C-3PO's skeletal form trembled. "Master Anakin, I don't think this is a good idea at all!"

As Anakin approached, the Tusken stirred, raising his head to look at Anakin, then lowered his head again.

He's still alive! From everything Anakin had heard about Tuskens, he knew it would be best to leave immediately. If he stuck around, more Tuskens might arrive. If he was late getting back to Mos Espa or failed to return with the droids and speeder, Watto would be furious. As C-3PO protested behind him, Anakin thought of his mother. He knew she'd be worried, but he wondered, *Would she tell me to get out of here too? What would she say, if she were here?*

"Threepio," he called to the nervous droid, "bring the other droids over here."

It took the combined strength of the various droids and the weight of the speeder to rig a lever that could tilt the boulder enough so Anakin could pull the now-unconscious Tusken free. Taking supplies from the speeder's medical kit, Anakin applied a quick-seal splint to freeze the Tusken's injured leg, which was broken in several places.

Tatooine's suns began to set. Anakin knew he'd never reach Mos Espa by nightfall, and he didn't want to risk traveling across the desert in the darkness. After doing his best to conceal the speeder and the newly purchased droids under the lee of a cliff face, Anakin sat beside C-3PO. Illuminated by a small glow unit they'd removed from the speeder, they were watching the Tusken Raider when he awoke. The Tusken lay on the sand, staring at Anakin through the opaque lenses of his goggles, then slowly raised himself to sit upright, taking care not to shift his injured leg.

"Uh, hello," Anakin said, hoping his voice sounded friendly.

The Tusken did not respond.

"Are you thirsty?"

Again, no response.

C-3PO leaned his one-eyed head closer to Anakin and said in a low voice, "I don't think he likes us very much."

The Tusken's head turned slightly. Anakin realized the Tusken had spotted his own blaster rifle, which Anakin had propped against some rocks beyond the Tusken's reach. Then the Tusken returned his gaze to Anakin.

Several minutes later, the Tusken spoke. Anakin didn't understand the snarled words, so he turned to C-3PO. The droid translated, "He wants to know what you are going to do with him, Master Anakin."

Confused, Anakin looked back at the Tusken. "Tell him I'm not going to do anything with him. I'm just trying to help him get well."

The Tusken didn't reply, but Anakin sensed he was afraid. Because nearly everyone believed Tusken Raiders to be fearless, Anakin was surprised. *Why's he afraid of me? I'm not afraid of him.* Then Anakin thought with some surprise, *I'm not afraid of anything.*

But as Anakin stared at the Tusken's masked face, he

saw his own reflection in the lenses of the Tusken's goggles, and shuddered slightly. He had heard that Tuskens never took off their masks or bared their flesh, and the thought of his entire body being so completely enveloped, sealed off so that he'd be unable to feel anything — *not even the touch of my mother's hand* — made Anakin suddenly realize a painful truth: Although he was never afraid for himself, he was sometimes very afraid for his mother.

What if I were to lose her? How brave would I be then?

Anakin continued watching the Tusken until he fell asleep.

Anakin Skywalker had many dreams that night. In one dream, he was no longer nine years old. He was a man. And not just any man, but a Jedi Knight with a lightsaber.

He ran through the streets of Mos Espa, looking for the few slavers who'd escaped him. His mission was to liberate all the slaves on Tatooine. For too long, slavers in the Outer Rim had believed themselves immune from the laws of the Galactic Republic. Anakin was going to change all that. He called out, "Release the slaves now and no harm will come to you!"

In the buildings that lined the streets of Mos Espa, some tenants leaned out of their windows and cheered for Anakin. Even though he'd deactivated his lightsaber's blade, most of the slavers were scared by the sight of him and his weapon, and surrendered when they saw him. Anakin gave them some credit for knowing better than to take on a Jedi.

A shadow snaked across the curved exterior of a nearby building. By the angle of the shadow, Anakin quickly determined that it was cast by a humanoid alien from atop a neighboring building's roof. From above and behind, Anakin heard the click of a blaster's safety mechanism being switched off. He thought, *Aha! A slaver who doesn't know better!*

Anakin's lightsaber ignited with a loud hum as he spun to look up at the roof, just in time to see the alien squeeze his blaster's trigger. Before the fired laserbolt could reach Anakin's chest, he swung hard with his lightsaber and smashed the bolt back at his attacker. The alien clutched at his shoulder and fell from the roof, landing with a loud thud on the sand-covered street. The dust was still settling when Anakin heard a woman's voice calling his name.

Anakin turned to see the woman. It was his mother, dressed in her rough work clothes. Anakin deactivated his lightsaber and said, "I came back, Mom! Like I promised! You're free!"

His mother smiled and opened her arms to Anakin. He ran to embrace her, but before he could reach her, she vanished. He was still clutching at the air where she'd been standing when he was suddenly surrounded by Sand People.

Anakin awoke with a start. Just as they had appeared in his dream, a group of Sand People now encircled him, silhouetted against the predawn sky. They carried blaster rifles and long gaffi sticks, double-edged axlike weapons made from metal scavenged from wrecked or abandoned vehicles. Anakin was completely at their mercy.

As he wondered what the Sand People would do to him, Anakin heard a guttural muttering from nearby. Beyond the group that stood around him, more Sand People were lifting and carrying away the Tusken that he'd rescued. The injured Tusken was the one who'd spoken, and his words caused the other Tuskens to slowly back away from Anakin.

Within seconds, all the Sand People were gone, leaving Anakin unharmed. *Maybe they were grateful to me for helping their friend. Maybe the Tuskens aren't so awful after all.*

"Master Anakin, they've gone!" C-3PO cried as he stepped away from his position beside the speeder, where he'd been hiding. "Oh, we're lucky to be alive! Thank goodness they didn't harm you!"

Anakin stood up and looked around. The speeder and the other droids were where he'd left them, but the injured Tusken's blaster rifle was gone. The only evidence of his encounter with the Sand People was the depleted contents of the speeder's medical kit and their footprints in the sand.

It's almost like the whole thing never happened.

As the twin suns began to rise and the stars faded from the brightening sky, Anakin decided it was time to head home.

His return to Mos Espa went as Anakin expected. After he'd snuck C-3PO back to Slave Quarters Row, his worried mother had nearly smothered him in hugs. When he delivered the droids to Watto, the angry Toydarian nearly lost his voice after bellowing reprimands for several minutes. Watto calmed down a bit after seeing the quality of the droids that Anakin had obtained from the Jawas, but by the end of the day, nothing had really changed. Tatooine was still a harsh, lawless world, and Anakin was still a slave.

The following day, however, something remarkable happened. That was the day a Naboo starship landed on Tatooine, and Anakin's life was forever changed.

CHAPTER FIVE

It was midday in Mos Espa, and Anakin was cleaning fan switches in Watto's junkyard when his master loudly summoned him into the junk shop to watch the store. Inside, Watto was talking with a tall, bearded man who was dressed like a farmer; the man was accompanied by a rubbery-jointed humanoid alien with mottled skin and eyes on the top of his head, a girl dressed in rough peasant clothes, and a dome-headed, blue astromech droid.

While the tall man and the astromech followed the hovering Watto to the scrap yard to look at engine parts, Anakin hitched himself up onto the counter that snaked through the shop and studied the girl. She had delicate features, her skin too perfect for a peasant. She appeared to be a few years older than him, and Anakin found himself unable to take his eyes off her.

"Are you an angel?" he blurted out.

She smiled — his heart soared — and said, "What?"

"An angel," he responded as she stepped closer to him. "I've heard the deep space pilots talk about them. They are the most beautiful creatures in the universe. They live on the Moons of Iego, I think."

"You're a funny little boy," she said sweetly. "How do you know so much?"

"I listen to all the traders and starpilots who come through here. I'm a pilot, you know, and someday, I'm going to fly away from this place."

"You're a pilot?" she said, as if she found it hard to believe.

"Mm-hmm. All my life."

"How long have you been here?"

"Since I was very little, three, I think. My mom and I were sold to Gardulla the Hutt, but she lost us, betting on the Podraces."

Sounding surprised and alarmed, the girl said, "You're a slave?"

Even though the girl had assumed correctly, Anakin didn't like being called a slave, and he felt stung by her question. "I'm a *person*," he said, glaring at her, "and my name is Anakin!"

"I'm sorry. I don't fully understand," the girl replied, and Anakin sensed she meant it. Unable to hold his gaze, she glanced around the shop's interior, as if seeking answers from the assorted scrap that lined the walls. "This is a strange place to me."

Anakin remembered his own arrival to Tatooine, and had to admit that he'd found it strange too. He tried to ignore the clumsy, mottled-skinned alien while he continued talking with the girl for a few more minutes, until the tall man and the astromech returned with Watto. The man announced that his group was leaving, and Anakin felt heartsick as the girl walked out the door.

After Watto gave Anakin permission to leave the shop, the boy caught up with the three outlanders and the astromech. When they learned a sandstorm was approaching, Anakin persuaded them to take temporary refuge in his home, where he introduced them to his mother and C-3PO. He discovered that the man was a Jedi Knight named Qui-Gon Jinn, the girl was fourteen-year-old Padmé Naberrie, the clumsy alien was a Gungan named Jar Jar Binks, and the astromech was R2-D2. When R2-D2 observed that the protocol droid, devoid of exterior plating, appeared to be naked, C-3PO became quite embarrassed.

Anakin had suspected that Qui-Gon Jinn was a Jedi even before the man admitted it in so many words. He had spotted Qui-Gon's lightsaber dangling from his belt on their way to Anakin's home, and he couldn't help wondering if Qui-Gon had come to Tatooine to free the slaves. Although Qui-Gon revealed few details about himself, Anakin could tell that he was a good and honorable man, the kind that had always been in short supply in Anakin's upbringing. Anakin admired the way Qui-Gon held himself with quiet confidence. When Jar Jar Binks made the mistake of using his own long tongue to snatch up a piece of food from the dining table, Anakin was both amused and amazed to see Qui-Gon's hand flash out with lightning speed to seize the Gungan's darting tongue with his thumb and forefinger.

"Don't do that again," Qui-Gon said with some severity before he released his grip and Jar Jar's tongue snapped back into his mouth.

Anakin thought, *Wizard!* Suddenly, he found himself wishing that Qui-Gon would teach him how to be a Jedi. But because Anakin had experienced enough disappointments in his life, it was difficult for him to imagine this could ever happen.

While Anakin and his mother sat with their new friends around the dining table, he told them of his dreams of becoming a Jedi. He learned that Padmé was a handmaiden to Queen Amidala of the planet Naboo, and that Qui-Gon had been escorting the queen and her entourage on an important mission to the planet Coruscant when their starship had been damaged, and they were forced to land on Tatooine without funds for the necessary repairs. Hoping to help, Anakin explained that a big Podrace, the Boonta Eve Classic, was scheduled for the following day. He volunteered to enter the race, which offered prize money that would more than pay for the parts they needed.

"Anakin!" Shmi protested. "Watto won't let you."

"Watto doesn't know I've built it." Turning to Qui-Gon, he said, "You could make him think it was yours, and get him to let me pilot it for you."

Although Padmé liked this idea about as much as Shmi did, Anakin was confident his plan — as well as his secret Podracer — would work.

The Boonta Eve Classic was the most dangerous race Anakin had ever flown in. It was a vicious, free-for-all competition, and more than one racer became victim to the high-speed turns, rocky obstacles, and dirty tricks of their dastardly adversaries.

The race's start had been difficult for Anakin. When he'd gunned his Podracer's engines at the starting signal, his turbines went dead, and he almost felt sick as he peered through his goggles to see the other pilots blasting off across the Starlite Flats, leaving him gasping in their dust. He'd lost precious seconds as he struggled with his controls, but when he finally managed to make the Radon-Ulzers fire, he threw his vehicle forward and launched out of Mos Espa Arena at top speed.

Soaring through the twisting chasms and over broad flats, Anakin managed to catch up with the other Podracers during the first lap. As the towering rock formations that dotted Mushroom Mesa whipped past him, he caught the scent of burning fuel a split second before he saw the scattered, smoking remains of the green-engined Pod that had been piloted by a Gran named Mawhonic. Somehow, he knew in his gut that Sebulba was responsible for the crash, and had no illusions that the Gran had survived.

Gripping his controls, Anakin gnashed his teeth and thought, *I'm not going to die like that!*

Anakin progressed at furious speed, maneuvering past several competitors as he sent his Podracer faster through the Boonta's exotic-named perils of Jag Crag Gorge, Laguna Caves, and Bindy Bend. While other pilots slowed slightly to negotiate the notoriously twisty chasm known as the Corkscrew, Anakin maintained a steady high speed until he arrived at Devil's Doorknob, a passage so narrow that pilots were required to flip their vehicles on their sides to travel through it. With expert skill beyond his years, he flipped his Pod to launch out of Devil's Doorknob, then accelerated to even greater speed over the broad expanse of the dead-sea bed known as Hutt Flats. Moments later, Mos Espa Arena came into view, and then he hurtled past the crowds who'd watched his delayed departure only minutes earlier.

There were still two laps to go.

Anakin knew he was rapidly gaining on the leading racers. As his Pod shot out of Beggar's Canyon, he caught sight of Mars Guo far up ahead, just behind Sebulba. Suddenly, one of Mars Guo's engines exploded, and a moment later, his Pod was flying in all directions.

Anakin plunged his own Pod dangerously close to the ground in a desperate effort to evade the fiery, airborne debris, but one large chunk of stray metal struck the steelton control cable that linked his Pod to his starboard engine. The control cable broke free, and Anakin's Pod — now linked only to the port engine — began spinning out of control.

Straining against the belts in his cockpit, Anakin tightened his neck muscles and clenched his teeth to prevent his head from snapping back. *Stay focused!* He sensed he was still traveling forward, and knew that the only reason he hadn't crashed so far was because the energy binder arc between the two engines had not yet failed.

As the surface of Tatooine blurred and spiraled around him, he punched at his cockpit controls until he stabilized the Pod, then reached for an emergency tool: his extendible magnetic retriever. He reached out with the tool, aiming its tip at the metal end of the starboard control cable that whipped and flailed alongside his cockpit. There was a satisfying *clank* as the magnetic retriever locked onto the cable's end. Anakin felt his arm strain as he pulled back on the cable, then he thrust the tool directly into the starboard cable socket. An instant later, he'd regained control of his ship.

Anakin didn't congratulate himself. His momentary loss of control had allowed the Xexto pilot Gasgano and a couple of other pilots to pass him, and Sebulba was still in the lead. Anakin did what he had to do: he kept going, only faster.

He swung around Gasgano, but as he attempted to pass the Veknoid pilot Teemto Pagalies, he felt a sudden bone-jarring jolt as Pagalies swerved to deliberately smack one of his long engines against Anakin's Pod. Anakin sat tight in his cockpit and stayed in control to lead Pagalies out of the Laguna Caves to emerge at the base of the wide, high-walled stretch called Canyon Dune Turn.

KRAK!

Despite the roar of his engines, Anakin heard the shot from above. A millisecond later, bright sparks flashed in front of him as fired projectiles pinged off his Pod. *Sand people! They're shooting at me!* He pushed his throttle levers, which sent him faster across the canyon. Anakin made it. Pagalies wasn't so fortunate.

Anakin caught up with Sebulba in the Corkscrew, but the cruel Dug flashed his engines directly in front of the young human. Anakin's Pod fell back, but he was still in second place as he followed Sebulba's Pod sideways out through Devil's Doorknob. Less than a minute later, Anakin followed Sebulba again through Mos Espa Arena.

Only one more lap!

Anakin kept on Sebulba's tail through the course, and was almost directly behind him when they began swerving through the narrow confines of Beggar's Canyon. Sebulba swung hard to the side, forcing Anakin off the course and onto the steep gradient of a service ramp. A moment later, Anakin's engines were carrying his Pod up and out of the canyon, launching him skyward.

No! Anakin thought. If he didn't win the race and the prize money, he wouldn't be able to help the Jedi buy the starship parts he needed to leave Tatooine. And he wanted very much to help the Jedi and the girl who traveled with him.

I can't lose!

When his Pod reached its maximum repulsorlift altitude, Anakin stayed calm as the vehicle arched back toward Tatooine's surface. Far below, he could see Sebulba's Pod still traveling through the canyon. Keeping his eyes on Sebulba's position, Anakin steered into a steep dive. He felt the air tear against his cheeks as he plunged back into the canyon, then angled his Pod and accelerated to position himself in front of the enraged Dug.

The thrill of being in the lead didn't last long. As Anakin and Sebulba headed through Jett's Chute on their way to the Corkscrew, Anakin's left engine overheated and began billowing smoke. The boy's nimble fingers quickly adjusted the controls to correct the malfunction, but as the two Pods blasted out of Devil's Doorknob and over the final stretch of Hutt Flats,

Sebulba began ramming Anakin from the side in a last nasty effort to force him out of the race.

Anakin thought, *He's crazy!*

The Dug slammed into Anakin again, but instead of knocking Anakin off course, the two Pods' steering rods became tangled and locked onto each other. Anakin glanced at Sebulba and saw the Dug frowning. If they remained locked in this position all the way over the finish line, the race would be a tie, but Anakin knew that would never happen. *Sebulba will either kill me or get us both killed before he'd allow a tie.*

Anakin jostled his throttle levers back and forth. *I have to break free.*

There was a loud *snap* as Anakin's Pod broke free from Sebulba's, and then the Dug's engines exploded. Sebulba shouted as his shattered Pod began crashing through the sand; Anakin swerved to avoid the debris, then accelerated for the finish line.

I did it! I won! I won! The crowd in the arena went wild.

After the race, a jubilant Anakin met with his mother, Padmé, Jar Jar, R2-D2, and C-3PO in the main hangar at the arena, where Watto had delivered the starship parts that Qui-Gon had requested. Anakin hadn't expected a celebration of his victory, but any hope of spending more time with his new friends ended when Qui-Gon showed up a few minutes later, looked to his traveling companions and said, "Let's go. We've got to get these parts back to the ship."

Anakin bit his lower lip. He wished he could leave Tatooine too, but knew it was pointless to say so. As Padmé and the others prepared to leave, he looked up at Qui-Gon, who said, "I have a few things to do before I leave. Go back home with your mother, and I'll meet you there in about an hour."

After returning home with Shmi and C-3PO and getting cleaned up, Anakin could not resist going outside to meet with some enthusiastic youngsters who'd seen him in the Boonta. He enjoyed their attention, and did his best to recount in detail the numerous hazards he'd encountered during the race. Most of the kids were very impressed. They listened attentively until a young Rodian, speaking in Huttese, said, "Too bad you didn't win fair and square."

Anakin glared at the Rodian and said, "You're calling me a cheater?"

"Yeah," the Rodian said. "No other way a human could've won. I'm guessing you probably —"

Before the Rodian could say another word, Anakin had knocked him to the sandy street. The other kids began shouting as Anakin straddled the Rodian and began punching him. Only a few blows had been exchanged before a long shadow appeared over both boys. Distracted, Anakin glanced up to see Qui-Gon standing beside him. A moment later, the Rodian shoved Anakin off of him.

Gazing down at Anakin, Qui-Gon said flatly, "What's this all about?"

"He said I cheated," Anakin glowered.

Keeping his eyes fixed on Anakin, Qui-Gon raised his eyebrows slightly and said, "Did you?"

Anakin was mildly outraged by the question. After all, Qui-Gon *knew* he hadn't cheated. Wondering why Qui-Gon didn't defend him, Anakin snapped, "No!"

Unruffled, Qui-Gon looked to the Rodian and asked, "Do you still think he cheated?"

In Huttese, the Rodian answered, "Yes, I do."

As Anakin pushed himself up from the ground, Qui-Gon said, "Well, Ani. You know the truth. You'll just have to tolerate his opinion. Fighting won't change it."

Maybe not, Anakin thought as he walked off with Qui-Gon, leaving the Rodian and the other kids behind. Still, he wasn't sure that tolerance was the best option. *If you don't defend your honor, no one will.* He wondered if Jedi ever had to defend their honor, but was reluctant to ask Qui-Gon. Even though the Jedi hadn't scolded him for fighting the Rodian, Qui-Gon had made it fairly obvious that he hadn't approved.

As they walked the short distance back to Anakin's home, Qui-Gon explained that repairs were already underway to Queen Amidala's starship, and that he'd sold Anakin's Pod. Handing a small pouch filled with credits to Anakin, Qui-Gon said, "Hey. These are yours."

Feeling the weight of the bag, Anakin exclaimed, "Yes!" Followed by Qui-Gon, he entered his home, where he found his mother sitting at her worktable. "Mom," he cried, "we sold the Pod! Look at all the money we have!"

"My goodness!" Shmi said as Anakin revealed the contents of the pouch he carried. "But that's so wonderful, Ani!"

Standing in the doorway, Qui-Gon added, "And he has been freed."

Anakin turned away from his mother and looked up at Qui-Gon. Wondering if he'd heard right, Anakin said, "What?"

"You're no longer a slave," Qui-Gon said.

Still slightly stunned by this unexpected news, Anakin looked back to his mother and said, "Did you hear that?"

"Now you can make your dreams come true, Ani," his mother said. "You are free." Then she sighed and looked down at the dirt floor.

Anakin thought his mother looked sad, and couldn't understand why she would be. Before he could ask, she turned her gaze to Qui-Gon and said, "Will you take him with you? Is he to become a Jedi?"

"Yes." Qui-Gon said. "Our meeting was not a coincidence. Nothing happens by accident."

Suspecting he really was dreaming, Anakin faced the Jedi and said, "You mean, *I* get to come with *you* in your starship?"

Kneeling down so he was almost eye-level with the boy, Qui-Gon said, "Anakin, training to become a Jedi is not an easy challenge, and even if you succeed, it's a hard life."

"But I wanna go!" Anakin said. "It's what I've always dreamed of doing." Turning away from Qui-Gon, he looked imploringly to his mother and said, "Can I go, Mom?"

Shmi smiled. "Anakin, this path has been placed before *you*. The choice is yours alone."

Anakin hesitated only a moment, then said, "I wanna do it."

"Then pack your things," Qui-Gon said. "We haven't much time."

"Yippee!" Anakin shouted as he ran toward his bedroom, but then he stopped dead as an awful realization suddenly occurred to him. Letting his gaze travel from Qui-Gon to his mother and back to the Jedi again, he said, "What about Mom? Is she free, too?"

"I tried to free your mother, Ani," Qui-Gon said, "but Watto wouldn't have it."

What? Anakin felt as if he'd been kicked. He walked slowly back to his mother and said, "You're coming with us, aren't you, Mom?"

Still seated beside her worktable, Shmi reached out and took Anakin's hands in hers. "Son, my place is here," she said. "My future is here. It is time for you to let go."

Anakin frowned. "I don't want things to change."

"But you can't stop the change," Shmi said, "any more than you can stop the suns from setting." Then she pulled her son close against her and hugged him tight. "Oh, I love you," she said. Precious seconds passed, then she held Anakin out at arm's length and said, "Now hurry." She gave his back a slight push before he trotted off to his bedroom, but without so much enthusiasm.

C-3PO's skeletal form had been deactivated and stood as silent and still as a statue as Anakin entered his room. Anakin flipped a switch on the droid's neck, and a moment later C-3PO's eyes winked on. "Oh!" the droid said, wobbling slightly as if he were surprised to find himself in a standing position. "Oh, my." Then he saw the boy. "Oh! Hello, Master Anakin."

As Anakin gathered up some of his belongings, he said, "Well, Threepio, I've been freed, and I'm going away in a starship."

"Master Anakin, you are my maker, and I wish you well. However, I should prefer it if I were a little more . . . completed."

"I'm sorry I wasn't able to finish you, Threepio, give you coverings and all," Anakin said as he stuffed some things into a travel sack. "I'm gonna miss working on you. You've been a great pal." Anakin slung the pack over his shoulder, then added, "I'll make sure Mom doesn't sell you or anything."

C-3PO's head recoiled slightly, and with genuine concern he said, "Sell me?"

"Bye," Anakin said as he left the room.

"Oh, my!" the droid exclaimed from behind.

Qui-Gon and Shmi watched Anakin emerge from his room. Suddenly, Anakin remembered the explosive implant within his body. He looked up at Qui-Gon and said, "Are you *sure* I'm not going to blow up when we leave Tatooine."

"I made sure that Watto deactivated the transmitter for your implant," Qui-Gon said. "When we reach our destination, we'll have the implant surgically removed."

"Okay, then," Anakin said. "I guess I'm as ready as I'll ever be."

Until the moment that Anakin led his mother and Qui-Gon outside the hovel, it hadn't occurred to him that he had no idea when he might return to Tatooine. *What if I never come back?* He suddenly felt like he was on remote, as if he were not in complete control of his own legs as they carried him into the harsh sunlight. It was hard to think clearly. Everything that had happened since the Jedi arrived on Tatooine seemed more like a dream than a reality.

He felt an awful ache in his chest as he said good-bye to his mother, but because he didn't want to disappoint

Qui-Gon, he tried not to make a big deal of the situation. He began to walk away with Qui-Gon, tried to concentrate on the path before him, but with each step, his legs felt increasingly heavy. He walked only a short distance when he stopped, then turned and ran back to his mother.

Shmi dropped to her knees and held Anakin tightly. Failing to fight back his tears, Anakin cried, "I can't do it, Mom. I just can't do it."

"Ani," Shmi said, holding him at arm's length so she could see his pained face.

"Will I ever see you again?" he sobbed.

"What does your heart tell you?"

Anakin tried to listen to his heart, but all he sensed was its ache. "I hope so," he said, then added, "Yes . . . I guess."

"Then we will see each other again."

Anakin swallowed hard. "I will come back and free you, Mom. I promise."

Shmi smiled. "Now be brave, and don't look back. *Don't look back.*"

Anakin did as his mother instructed, lowering his gaze to the sand-packed street as he followed Qui-Gon away from the hovels. Each step was an effort to stay balanced, as if he could not completely trust his legs from stopping or turning him back toward his mother. He trudged forward, trying to keep up with Qui-Gon's measured strides. He choked back a sob and felt his throat go dry. Thanks to the arid air, he did not have to wipe away his tears, for they evaporated faster than he could cry.

Making their way out of Mos Espa, Qui-Gon and Anakin stopped briefly at the market place so Anakin could say good-bye to his friend Jira, an old woman who sold fruits called pallies. Seated behind her small fruit stand, Jira's weathered face brightened at Anakin's approach. Anakin announced, "I'm free." Before Jira could comment, he handed her some of his winnings and said, "Here. Buy yourself a cooling unit with this or else I'll worry about you."

Astonished, Jira gaped for a moment, then said, "Can I give you a hug?"

"Sure," Anakin said as he leaned in close to Jira.

"Oh, I'll miss you, Ani," Jira said as she released him. "You're the kindest boy in the galaxy." Beaming, she wagged a finger at him and added, "You take care."

"Okay," Anakin said. "I will. Bye." He trudged off with Qui-Gon.

Anakin and Qui-Gon were at the very outskirts of Mos Espa when Anakin had a strange feeling . . . *Like we're being followed*. He doubted that the feeling was worth mentioning, but a moment later, Qui-Gon stopped fast and spun as he activated and swung his lightsaber at something behind them. Once again amazed by the Jedi's speed, Anakin gasped as the lightsaber swept through a spherical black repulsorlift device that had been hovering in the air at their backs.

Neatly halved, the shattered contraption fell to the sand. Qui-Gon bent down to examine the parts as they sizzled and sparked.

Anakin said, "What is it?"

"A probe droid," Qui-Gon said. "Very unusual. Not like anything I've seen before."

Anakin had heard of probe droids before. They resembled security droids, which were engineered to watch over places, but their specialized sensors and programming were more for spying. He'd heard rumors that some probe droids were equipped with weapons, and that the Hutts used them as assassins.

Glancing around for any sign of the probe droid's unknown owner, Qui-Gon rose quickly and said, "Come on." He turned and began to run, leading Anakin away from Mos Espa and into the desert wastes.

Anakin did his best to keep up with the tall Jedi as they raced over the dunes. But by the time Anakin sighted Queen Amidala's long, sleek starship just up ahead of them, he was trailing some distance behind the Jedi. Anakin had never seen a ship like it. Its surface was so highly reflective that it was literally blinding in the sunlight, and Anakin had to squint to look at it directly. As he fell farther behind Qui-Gon, he feared he'd never reach that beautiful ship.

"Qui-Gon, sir, wait!" Anakin yelled as he trudged forward across the shifting sand. "I'm tired!"

Qui-Gon spun and Anakin thought the Jedi was

looking at him, but then heard the hum of an engine approaching from behind. Qui-Gon shouted, "Anakin! Drop!"

Without hesitation, Anakin threw himself down upon the sand just as a scythe-shaped speeder swept past him. Anakin lifted his gaze to see a black-clad figure ignite a red-bladed lightsaber and leap from the speeder. As the speeder hurtled forward without its rider, Qui-Gon activated his own lightsaber just in time to block a strike from his deadly assailant.

"Go!" Qui-Gon shouted to Anakin. "Tell them to take off!"

Again, Anakin obeyed the Jedi without question. As he got up and ran, he caught but a glimpse of the dark warrior's face, which was covered with jagged red and black markings. Anakin didn't stop to ponder whether one color was the creature's skin color and the other was tattooed. He just kept running. And as tired as he was from the long run from Mos Espa, he never ran faster than he did when he bolted for the starship. He practically flew up the landing ramp and into the ship's forward hold. Just inside the hatchway, he found Padmé talking to a tall man in a leather tunic.

"Qui-Gon's in trouble!" Anakin blurted out between gasps. "He says to take off! Now!"

The man scowled at Anakin and demanded." Who are you?"

"He's a friend," Padmé answered for Anakin as she grabbed the breathless boy's arm and led him to the ship's bridge. The man followed them as they entered the bridge, where two other men — an older fellow in a pilot uniform, and a younger man in a robe — were checking the controls.

"Qui-Gon's in trouble," said the man who had followed Padmé and Anakin.

The young man in the robe hunkered down beside the pilot and said, "Take off." Then he peered through the ship's viewport, pointed and said, "Over there. Fly low."

Anakin stood behind the robed man and followed his gaze to see Qui-Gon dueling the dark warrior. In the short time he'd known Qui-Gon, Anakin had come to regard the Jedi as an invincible being, but now, he genuinely feared for Qui-Gon's life.

The ship's engines fired, then it lifted from the ground and began moving through the air toward Qui-Gon's position. Anakin held his breath as they passed over the fighting figures, then glanced at a monitor that displayed the forward hold. A moment later, Qui-Gon rolled into the hold and collapsed against the floor. Anakin realized Qui-Gon had leaped to the ship's still-extended landing ramp. *He made it!*

The robed man ran from the bridge to the forward hold and Anakin followed. Qui-Gon was still catching his breath as he introduced Anakin to his Jedi apprentice, Obi-Wan Kenobi.

*   *   *

Anakin's departure from Tatooine was followed by a dizzying series of events: his arrival on the skyscraper-covered world of Coruscant, home of the Galactic Senate and the Jedi Temple; his meeting with Yoda, Mace Windu, and the other members of the Jedi High Council, who tested his abilities with the power that they called the Force; the Council's subsequent rejection of Qui-Gon's request to train Anakin to become a Jedi, even though Qui-Gon insisted that Anakin was the "chosen one." Anakin's mind spun. *Chosen one? Chosen for what?*

Before Anakin could begin to fully comprehend his situation, he was traveling again with Qui-Gon and Obi-Wan, as they escorted the ornately attired Queen Amidala back to Naboo, which had been invaded by the droid armies of the Neimoidian Trade Federation. On Naboo, Anakin was stunned to discover that Padmé Naberrie had impersonated a handmaiden for security reasons, and that she was really Padmé Amidala, the true Queen of Naboo.

Suddenly swept up into the battle between the Trade Federation's droids and the inhabitants of Naboo, Anakin had just taken refuge in a starfighter cockpit when Qui-Gon and Obi-Wan were confronted by the same dark warrior who'd appeared on Tatooine. Although Anakin had not intended to commandeer the starfighter to destroy the large ship that controlled the Federation's droids, his actions brought a swift end to the invasion.

After the battle, Anakin found Obi-Wan at the queen's palace. From Obi-Wan's grim expression, Anakin knew what had happened. Qui-Gon Jinn was dead.

Three days later, the Jedi Council honored Qui-Gon's final wish, and allowed Anakin to become Obi-Wan's apprentice. When Anakin realized that even the newly appointed Supreme Chancellor Palpatine, the former Senator of Naboo, was aware of his role in destroying the droid control ship, he thought he'd gone as far as a slave from Tatooine ever could.

But his adventures were only beginning.

Darth Vader never pondered what might have happened if Qui-Gon Jinn had not discovered young Anakin Skywalker, or if Anakin had not won that crucial Podrace. Nor did he wonder whether Anakin's life might have taken a different path if Qui-Gon — instead of Obi-Wan Kenobi — had survived the duel with the Sith Lord Darth Maul on Naboo. On Tatooine, Qui-Gon had asserted that nothing happened by accident, and although there were many things that Vader would have disagreed upon with Qui-Gon, he would have agreed with this, because Vader believed in destiny.

He believed it had been Anakin's destiny to leave Tatooine and become a Jedi, just as he had been destined for everything that had happened after that. It was pointless to speculate how his life might have been different.

Now, still en route to Endor, the black-masked Dark Lord wondered if Luke Skywalker had any illusions about being able to control his own destiny. Vader thought, If he fights me, he will fail.

Still, Vader would have been almost disappointed if Luke were to surrender too soon, without any effort to resist the power of the dark side. After all, Anakin Skywalker had been a young man once, and he had not surrendered easily. . . .

CHAPTER SIX

As a Padawan apprentice to Obi-Wan Kenobi, Anakin Skywalker was eager to become a Jedi Knight. However, the hallowed halls of the Jedi Temple did not encourage eagerness, and the Jedi Masters insisted that Anakin devote himself to serious study of the Force and the history of the Jedi.

He learned about the nature of the Force, the energy field that was generated by all living things, and which suffused and bound the entire galaxy together. Ancient Jedi had learned to manipulate the Force and chose to use it selflessly to help others. They identified two sides to the Force: the light side, which bestowed great knowledge, peace, and serenity; and the dark side, which was filled with fear, anger, and aggression. Long ago, a group of Jedi had turned to the dark side and were exiled to an unknown region of space, where they came to dominate the Sith species and to call themselves Sith Lords. Jedi investigators concluded that Qui-Gon Jinn's killer was a

Sith Lord, the first to appear in Republic space for a thousand years.

Anakin also learned about *midi-chlorians*, microscopic life-forms found in all living things, which could determine the scope of a Jedi's powers. A blood test had determined that Anakin's body contained more midi-chlorians than any known Jedi, even the great Jedi Master Yoda, which led some Jedi to believe that he had the potential to become the most powerful Jedi ever.

The Jedi Archives were filled with many Jedi Holocrons, ancient devices that projected holograms and served as interactive educational tools, and it was through the Holocrons that Anakin learned more about the prophecy of the Chosen One, a Jedi who would destroy the Sith and bring balance to the Force. He could only imagine the ramifications of the prophecy, but he felt very, very proud as he recalled how Qui-Gon Jinn had told the Jedi Council that he believed Anakin was the Chosen One.

But Anakin was also bitter that he had not been *chosen* by Obi-Wan, who had only accepted him as an apprentice out of obligation to Qui-Gon. Because Anakin had not been trained since infancy at the Temple like nearly all other Padawans, various Jedi Masters accepted the fact that he lacked the discipline of his fellow students. They were less accepting, however, of his arrogant behavior when he demonstrated his abilities.

I'm more powerful with the Force than some of my instructors, Anakin thought, *and they know it!*

Like eagerness, pride and arrogance were not acceptable characteristics for any Jedi, even if he really did turn out to be the Chosen One. Many Jedi remained cautious of him.

They're just jealous.

Anakin enjoyed praise from Obi-Wan, but often became sullen when he was reprimanded. Obi-Wan assured him that he himself had been frequently reminded by Qui-Gon to be more mindful of the Force, but somehow even the slightest criticism managed to leave Anakin feeling stung.

First they tell me to do my best, then they tell me I've gone too far!

Obi-Wan was sympathetic. He knew that Anakin's upbringing — as well as his formidable powers — set him apart from the other Padawans and even alienated him from some of the Jedi Masters. After all, Anakin had an unfortunate history with the word "Master."

They don't know what it's like to be born into slavery.

He also had difficulty adjusting to an environment that discouraged anger as well as love, as such emotions could cloud a Jedi's judgment and lead to negative thoughts and actions. The boy could no sooner forget his mother than he could stop loving her. Nor could he stop missing her, or resenting the fact that the Jedi order discouraged contact with relatives.

Why won't they help me free my mother? It's not fair! It's not right!

Countless times, Obi-Wan explained that every Jedi had to obey the directives of the Jedi Council, and could never use the Force for selfish purposes. He urged Anakin to consider how freeing one slave on Tatooine might lead to the deaths of others, as some slavers might prefer to destroy their "property" than release them from bondage. The Jedi also had to answer to the Galactic Senate, and for the time being, the Senate had little interest in anything that happened on Tatooine.

Why do the Jedi have to answer to anybody? Anakin wondered.

Despite Anakin's desire to distance himself from the slave he had once been, he was unable, or unwilling, to shed the other aspects that had defined him on Tatooine. He still dreamed of glory, still craved adventure, and never lost his appetite for high-speed thrills and the desire to prove himself in competition.

Over the years, Anakin's actions often tested his master's patience. At age twelve, he flew in illegal garbage pit races in the bowels of Galactic City on Coruscant. When he was nearly thirteen, he constructed his first lightsaber, which he soon used to bring about the end of a notorious slaver named Krayn. At fifteen, while on a mission with Obi-Wan to serve as peacekeepers at the Galactic Games on the planet Euceron, he competed in an illegal Podrace to win the freedom of a slave. At seventeen, his rivalry with another Padawan led to a most unfortunate outcome on the ancient Sith home-world of Korriban. Later that year, unusual circum-stances led him to enter a Podrace against his childhood nemesis, Sebulba, on Ryloth.

Eventually, Anakin realized that Obi-Wan was the one Jedi who refused to give up on him. He came to regard Obi-Wan as the father figure he never had, although Qui-Gon Jinn had certainly come close in that area. In time, Anakin and Obi-Wan learned to trust each other and became close friends. As with Obi-Wan's former partnership with Qui-Gon, they gained a reputation as a capable team, so attuned that they could sense each oth-er's presence across great distances. Although they were most often called upon for diplomatic missions, they were also dispatched on many dangerous assignments.

Much to Anakin's surprise, Supreme Chancellor Palpatine took a special interest in him and his activi-ties. Time and again, Palpatine told Anakin that he was the most gifted Jedi he'd ever met, and that he envisioned Anakin would someday become even more powerful than Master Yoda.

But for all of Anakin's confidence in his powers, all his accomplishments and victories, and all the lessons learned in the decade that followed the Battle of Naboo, nothing prepared him, at age twenty, for his reunion with Padmé Amidala.

                              *   *   *

"Ani?" said Padmé, taken aback at the sight of the
tall young man who stood beside Obi-Wan in her apartment on Coruscant. The two Jedi had just returned from
a mission to resolve a border dispute on Ansion when
they'd been instructed to meet with Padmé, who had
continued to serve her homeworld as a Galactic Senator
after completing her second term as the elected Queen
of Naboo. Also present in the apartment were Jar Jar Binks
and a Naboo security officer. Padmé and Jar Jar had not
seen Obi-Wan and Anakin in ten years, and Padmé
beamed at Anakin as she said, "My goodness, how
you've grown."

Hoping to sound mature, Anakin replied without
thinking, "So have you." *What a stupid thing to say. The
last time I saw her, I was shorter than her!* Hoping to
recover from his embarrassment, he added, "Grown
more beautiful, I mean." *Did I just say that?* "Well, f-for
a Senator, I mean." *Everyone in this room must think
I'm an idiot!*

Padmé laughed, "Ani, you'll always be that little
boy I knew on Tatooine."

Anakin felt crushed. He'd thought of Padmé every
day since their first encounter, and he didn't want her to
think of him as "that little boy."

She's even more beautiful than I remembered.

Although the old friends were glad to see each other
again, the circumstances of their reunion were grave.

The Galactic Senate had grown so corrupt that the citizens of many worlds were threatening to end their allegiance to the Republic and create their own government. A former Jedi, the charismatic Count Dooku, had begun to organize this Separatist movement, and many believed the situation would erupt into an all-out civil war. Because the Jedi order was unprepared for such a massive conflict, many Senators wanted to create an army to defend and preserve the Republic.

Hoping to find a peaceful resolution, Senator Amidala had traveled to Coruscant to cast her vote against the Military Creation Act, but was nearly assassinated upon her arrival. In a terrifying ambush, her starship was destroyed and six people, including one of her bodyguards, were killed. At Supreme Chancellor Palpatine's request, Obi-Wan and Anakin had been appointed to protect Padmé.

To make matters worse, in recent weeks, Anakin had been disturbed by a series of dreams that his mother was in danger. He considered whether the dreams had been some kind of premonition of the attack on Padmé, but sensed that the visions were unrelated. In the most startling nightmare, his mother had been transformed into a glass statue and shattered before his eyes. *It was just a bad dream*, Anakin tried to convince himself as he focused on his assignment.

It was Padmé's idea to use herself as bait to lure the mysterious assassin into the hands of the Jedi.

Hearing her plan, Anakin said, "It's a bad . . . I mean, it's not a good idea, Senator." Beside him, R2-D2 beeped in what may have been an agreement. Although Anakin had been secretly happy to have had this moment alone with Padmé in her apartment, he almost wished Obi-Wan were with them right now, instead of meeting with the Jedi Council, so that he could discourage Padmé, too.

Padmé said, "Moving me to a different suite will only delay another attack."

"But what you're suggesting is far too dangerous. You could get hurt."

"That *is* a possibility," Padmé said. "But if we prepare for an attack here in this suite, and really cover every angle, then we would have an advantage over the assassin, wouldn't we? And Artoo can help . . ."

Looking away from Padmé, Anakin shook his head and said, "It would still be too risky. For all we know, there may be a whole army of assassins."

Padmé stepped closer to Anakin, forcing him to turn back to her and meet her gaze. She said, "I have no interest in dying, Anakin, but I don't want any more innocent people to lose their lives because someone wants me dead. If you can understand that, then you'll help me do this."

As much as Anakin wanted to apprehend the people who had tried to kill Padmé, he knew that Obi-Wan would not readily approve the idea of using Padmé as bait. Despite his better judgment, Anakin said, "All right, Senator. I'll help you."

Obi-Wan didn't learn about the plan until later that evening, when Padmé was already asleep. Despite their preparations and the watchful presence of R2-D2, Obi-Wan and Anakin had to move fast to intercept the pair of kouhuns — small, deadly arthropods — that invaded the sleeping Senator's apartment and stealthily slithered their way onto her bed. The Jedi had to move even faster to catch up with the assassin who'd unleashed the kouhuns.

Traveling by airspeeder and instinct, the Jedi pursued their quarry for more than 100 kilometers through the skies and streets of Galactic City before their hunt ended in a crowded nightclub. Although the assassin appeared to be a fair-skinned female human, she was actually a Clawdite shapeshifter who wore a dark elastic bodysuit that remained taut when she changed forms. Inside the nightclub, her attempt to shoot Obi-Wan in the back had resulted in the Jedi using his lightsaber to literally disarm her. The Clawdite was still in shock as Obi-Wan carried her through an exit that led to an alley outside the club. Anakin walked alongside them, and the look of simmering rage in his eyes was all the power he needed to encourage the local denizens to clear the alley.

The Clawdite moaned as Obi-Wan eased her trembling body onto the alley floor. Anakin hoped she would stay conscious long enough to provide some answers. Obi-Wan looked into the Clawdite's eyes and said, "Do you know who it was you were trying to kill?"

"It was a senator from Naboo," the Clawdite muttered.

"And who hired you?"

The muscles in her face spasmed as she tried to maintain a human visage. She muttered, "It was just a job."

Kneeling beside the Clawdite, Anakin felt his anger rise at this creature who considered killing Padmé "just a job." It took all of his self-control to maintain a calm, gentle tone as he leaned forward and asked, "Who hired you? Tell us."

The Clawdite's eyes rolled toward Anakin. When she didn't answer immediately, Anakin roared, "Tell us now!"

The Clawdite gulped, then said, "It was a bounty hunter called —"

Her statement was interrupted by a small projectile that made a *ftzzz* sound as it streaked down and embedded itself in her neck. Anakin and Obi-Wan turned their heads fast and traced the projectile's trajectory to a high upper roof, where an armored man wearing a jetpack suddenly launched into the sky and disappeared.

The two Jedi looked back to the Clawdite, whose flesh turned dark green as her features contorted back to their natural configuration. "Wee shahnit . . . sleemo," she gasped before her head tilted back.

Being fluent in Huttese, Anakin understood the assassin's last words: *bounty hunter slimeball*. And with great bitterness, he wished she had given them a name instead.

Obi-Wan reached to the dead Clawdite's neck and removed the projectile, a nasty little item that had stabilizing fins for long-range shooting and an injector-needle tip. "Toxic dart," Obi-Wan observed.

Anakin felt some relief that at least one assassin could no longer harm Padmé. Looking at the Clawdite's corpse, he thought, *You got what you deserved.*

And then he trembled. He knew it wasn't the way of the Jedi to think anyone *deserved* to die.

But he'd thought it just the same.

CHAPTER SEVEN

Because Senator Amidala was still in danger, the Jedi Council instructed Obi-Wan to track down the elusive bounty hunter while Anakin escorted Padmé back to Naboo. To prevent anyone from knowing Padmé's whereabouts, she and Anakin disguised themselves as refugees and left with R2-D2 aboard a starfreighter for the Naboo system. Anakin remained extremely concerned for Padmé's safety, but he was also secretly delighted that his mission — his first official assignment without his Master — would allow him to spend more time with the young woman he had adored since childhood.

Is it possible she has feelings for me too? he couldn't stop wondering.

Inside the Naboo-bound starfreighter, they kept to themselves among the emigrants in the steerage hold. Anakin chanced a nap during the long flight, but was visited by another nightmare. In his sleep, he muttered, "No, no, Mom, no . . . ," then woke with a start. Padmé hovered near, looking at him. Somewhat confused, he returned her gaze and said, "What?"

"You seemed to be having a nightmare."

Anakin didn't comment. But later, while sharing a meal of mush and bread, Padmé persisted. "You were dreaming about your mother earlier, weren't you?"

"Yes," Anakin admitted. "I left Tatooine so long ago, my memory of her is fading. I don't want to lose it. Recently, I've been seeing her in my dreams . . . vivid dreams . . . scary dreams. I worry about her."

Just then, R2-D2 moved over to them and emitted an electronic whistle. The starfreighter had arrived in the Naboo system.

Anakin accompanied Padmé everywhere on Naboo, and soon met her family. At first, Padmé treated her Jedi guardian like a slightly unwelcome shadow that followed her every movement. She seemed as determined to withhold personal information as he was to discover it, and denied to her own sister that her relationship with Anakin was anything other than professional.

But as the days passed, she became more relaxed in the presence of the young man who was constantly at her side, and their conversations changed from her devotion to politics and his concerns regarding security to more intimate subjects. As for Anakin, he learned about Padmé's cherished memories of children she'd known as a relief worker, and her favorite places on Naboo.

Because Anakin had grown up under the sweltering suns of Tatooine, he'd felt cold on most of the worlds he'd visited, but with Padmé on Naboo, he felt — for the first time in his life — truly comfortable. And happy.

They were standing on the garden terrace at a lodge that overlooked a lake, and Padmé was wearing a gown that revealed the fair skin of her back and arms when Anakin cautiously leaned close to her face and kissed her. She did not resist, but several seconds after their lips met, she pulled away from him and said, "No." She looked away, fixing her eyes on the lake before them.

"I shouldn't have done that," she said.

Anakin had been aching to kiss her since their reunion on Coruscant, but he'd never planned on it, let alone imagined that he ever actually would. Padmé's acceptance and return of his kiss had been his greatest moment of joy, and to be so suddenly rejected left him feeling devastated, embarrassed, and confused. He followed her gaze to the tranquil waters and said, "I'm sorry."

I'm sorry you don't feel the same way for me that I do for you.

Anakin tried to pretend the kiss had never happened. But with every minute that passed after that moment by the lake, every moment spent with Padmé, he felt more tortured, as if his heart had become an open wound. Unable to wish his feelings away, he confronted Padmé, who reminded him that Jedi were not allowed to marry, and that she was a Senator who had more important things to do than fall in love. When Anakin suggested that they might maintain a secret relationship, she told him that she refused to live a lie.

Anakin began wondering about his place in the Jedi order. The more he thought about all the rules to follow and the time devoted to meditation and training, the more he questioned the logic of so much personal sacrifice. *Is it so wrong that I care for Padmé as much as I do? Or that I still miss my mother and worry about her?* For the first time since he'd become a Jedi, he found himself seriously considering the possibility of relinquishing his lightsaber, leaving the order, and becoming a citizen of the galaxy.

He tried to imagine himself in another career. He was confident that he could find work as a pilot or a mechanic. *But would doing that sort of work make me happy?* The answer came immediately to Anakin: the *only* thing that would make him happy was to be with Padmé.

But what if I stopped being a Jedi and she still didn't see any chance of a future with me? What then? It was all too overwhelming to contemplate.

While Anakin's waking moments had become emotionally painful, sleeping was even worse. One morning, he was standing on a balcony at the lodge, meditating with his eyes closed, when he sensed Padmé's approach from behind.

"You had another nightmare last night," she said.

"Jedi don't have nightmares," he replied tersely.

"I *heard* you."

Anakin didn't doubt that she had. The nightmare had been the worst one yet. He opened his eyes and said, "I saw my mother." Turning to face Padmé, he fought to keep his voice from trembling. "She's suffering, Padmé. I saw her as I see you now." He let out a long sigh, barely releasing the pressure that was building up within him. He feared that last night's dream was not a premonition, but a vision of events that had already transpired. "She's in pain," he continued. "I know I'm disobeying my mandate to protect you, Senator, but I have to go. I have to help her!"

"I'll go with you," Padmé said.

"I'm sorry," Anakin said. "I don't have a choice."

He hadn't expected the possibility that she might go with him to Tatooine. *I can continue to watch her. Obi-Wan wouldn't approve, but . . . it's not his decision.*

Without notifying Obi-Wan or the Jedi Council of his plans, Anakin, Padmé, and R2-D2 left Naboo in a slim H-type Nubian yacht. The fragrant scents of Padmé's lush, fertile homeworld were still fresh in Anakin's nostrils when he sighted the scorched, barren sand planet.

Descending through the atmosphere, they flew to the Mos Espa spaceport. After landing and securing the ship in one of the deep, open pits that served as landing bays, Anakin hired a droid-powered rickshaw to carry him and Padmé to Watto's junk shop. R2-D2 motored along behind them.

Anakin wasn't sure how he'd react when he saw Watto again. Although his former master had been kinder than other slave owners, Anakin had always resented the fact that Watto refused to free his mother. *Watto isn't entirely to blame*, Anakin mused, wondering just how hard Qui-Gon had tried to liberate Shmi. *Slavery is allowed here, and Watto is just a businessman.*

Soon they reached Watto's shop, where they found the old Toydarian seated out front. Not surprisingly, Watto did not recognize the tall young Jedi who stood before him, but when Anakin said he was looking for Shmi Skywalker, Watto made the connection.

"Ani?" Watto gasped in disbelief. "Little Ani? Nahhh!" His eyes went wide, then he flapped his wings and shouted, "You are Ani! It is you! You sure sprouted, huh?"

Watto then informed Anakin that he'd sold Shmi years earlier to a moisture farmer named Lars, and that he'd heard Lars had freed and married Shmi. Fortunately, Watto's records provided the location of the moisture farm, which was near a small community called Anchorhead.

After returning to their starship and blasting out of the landing bay, Anakin, Padmé, and R2-D2 soared high over the northern Dune Sea. It was only a matter of minutes before they touched down at the edge of the farm, which consisted of moisture-collecting vaporators spread out around a small, domed structure. The dome was an entrance to an underground homestead and an adjoining courtyard that rested in an open pit. R2-D2 stayed with the ship while Anakin and Padmé walked toward the dome. Once there, they were greeted by a fully plated protocol droid.

"Oh!" exclaimed the droid when he noticed the two humans approaching. The droid had been making a minor adjustment to a binocular Treadwell droid, but now turned to face Anakin and Padmé. "Um, uh, hello. How might I be of service? I am C —"

"Threepio?" Anakin said, wondering if his mother had been responsible for putting the metal coverings on the droid's body.

Confused, C-3PO tilted his head slightly. "Oh, um . . ." Then it hit him. "The maker! Oh, Master Ani! I knew you would return. I knew it! And Miss Padmé. Oh, my."

C-3PO led them down a flight of steps to the courtyard, where a surprised young man and woman emerged through an arched doorway. The couple wore drab desert robes that were common on the sand planet. The man was sturdily built, with strong farmer's hands.

C-3PO said, "Master Owen, might I present two most important visitors."

"I'm Anakin Skywalker," Anakin said.

"Owen Lars," Owen said, sounding slightly unnerved. Gesturing to the woman beside him, he said, "Uh, this is my girlfriend, Beru."

Beru smiled shyly, and exchanged greetings with Padmé.

Keeping his eyes on Anakin, Owen continued, "I guess I'm your stepbrother. I had a feeling you might show up someday."

Anxious and impatient, Anakin scanned the courtyard and said, "Is my mother here?"

"No, she's not," answered a deep voice from behind. Anakin and Padmé turned to see an older man whose grizzled features betrayed that he was obviously Owen's father. He was seated in a hovering mechno-chair, and his robe was pulled back to reveal that his right leg was a bandaged stump. "Cliegg Lars," he introduced himself as his chair carried him slowly forward. "Shmi is my wife. We should go inside. We have a lot to talk about."

A few minutes later, in the hollowed-out dining chamber, Anakin and Padmé were seated at a rectangular table with Cliegg and Owen. "It was just before dawn," Cliegg recounted. "They came out of nowhere. A hunting party of Tusken Raiders."

Anakin felt his stomach clench.

As Beru set a tray of beverages on the table, Cliegg continued, "Your mother had gone out early, like she always did, to pick mushrooms that grow on the vaporators. From the tracks, she was about halfway home when they took her. Those Tuskens walk like men, but they're vicious, mindless monsters. Thirty of us went out after her. Four of us came back. I'd be with them, but after I lost my leg . . . I just couldn't ride anymore . . . un-until I heal."

Anakin lowered his gaze to the untouched beverages on the table. His facial muscles twitched nervously as he thought, *If only she'd left Tatooine with me. If only I hadn't left her behind. . . .* Anakin hadn't had much time to develop an opinion about Cliegg Lars. Initially, he had felt some sense of gratitude to the man who'd helped liberate his mother from Watto. But because Cliegg had taken his wife to live in this desolate area where Tuskens roamed, Anakin couldn't help feeling a bitter anger. *If only* you *hadn't brought her* here!

"I don't want to give up on her," Cliegg said, "but she's been gone a month. There's little hope she's lasted this long."

Making every effort to control his rage, Anakin rose and stepped away from the table.

"Where are you going?" Owen asked.

Anakin shot an accusatory glare at Owen and replied, "To find my mother."

CHAPTER EIGHT

The suns were beginning to set as Anakin stood outside the entry dome at the Lars family homestead. Owen had offered his swoop bike to Anakin, and the bike was now parked in the air a short distance from the dome. *I shouldn't be angry with Owen and Cliegg for giving up*, Anakin thought. *They cared for my mother, but they're only human. They can only do so much.*

Padmé emerged from the entry dome and went to Anakin. He knew she wanted to help, but he also knew there wasn't any way he was going to risk her life any more than he already had. "You're gonna have to stay here," he said. "These are good people, Padmé. You'll be safe."

"Anakin —"

They embraced. Anakin almost wished he could have frozen that moment, just to keep Padmé forever close to him. But darkness was coming up fast, and his mother was still out there somewhere. *She's alive*, he felt. *I know she is!*

Releasing himself from Padmé's arms, Anakin walked to the swoop bike. "I won't be long," he said. He swung himself onto the bike, fired the engine, and tore off across the desert floor.

With the hot wind whipping at his robe, Anakin crossed into the Jundland Wastes, where Tusken Raiders were known to hide and hunt among the towering rock formations. He didn't wonder why the Tuskens had taken his mother, or why they hadn't killed her as they had the other farmers. For all he knew, the Tuskens were acting out some profane ritual. Their motives were not his concern. He just wanted his mother back.

He also wanted her back in one piece. He thought about what the Tuskens had done to Cliegg Lars, and he launched the bike faster over the Wastes.

He was about 150 kilometers from the Lars homestead when he sighted the tall silhouettes of sandcrawlers against the twilight sky. It was a Jawa camp. Although Jawas feared Tusken Raiders as much as anyone on Tatooine, Anakin knew the small, glowing-eyed scavengers would be more willing to provide information if he gave something in return. In exchange for a multitool and a portable scanner that he found in his borrowed bike's pannier, the Jawas told him he should head east to find a Tusken camp.

Tatooine's suns had long since set and the moons hung low over the horizon when Anakin saw the cluster of flickering campfires at the bottom of a deep valley. Leaving the swoop bike on the edge of a high cliff, he kept to the shadows as he ventured down into the valley and moved silently toward the camp.

The camp consisted of about two dozen tents made of skins and salvaged bits of wood from Tatooine's long-dead forests. Two Tuskens stood a short distance from one tent, guarding it. Anakin reached out with the Force and sensed his mother was inside. Without drawing any attention to himself, he maneuvered around to the back of the tent, used his lightsaber to cut a hole through the taut skin covering, and stepped inside.

Anakin found his mother at the center of the tent, tied to a frame made of thin wooden sticks. A small fire burned in a nearby pot and cast warm, wicked shadows across the tent walls. Shmi wasn't moving.

Scared as a child, Anakin said, "Mom?"

No response. He could see from the dried blood on her face and arms that she'd been terribly beaten. "Mom?" Still no response. She was barely alive. She moaned as he slipped her wrists free from the leather strips that had bound her to the frame. He gently lowered her to the ground, cradling her upper body in his arms. "Mom?"

Shmi's bruised eyelids fluttered open, and she struggled to focus on Anakin's face. "Ani?" she muttered. "Is it you?"

"I'm here, Mom," he said. "You're safe."

"Ani? Ani?" She seemed confused, as if she were trying to figure out whether he really was there. Then, incredibly, she managed to smile at him. "Oh, you look so handsome." She brushed her hand against his face, and he kissed her open palm. "My son. Oh, my grown-up son. I'm so proud of you, Ani."

Anakin swallowed hard and felt the sting of tears in his eyes as he said, "I missed you."

"Now I am complete," Shmi said. "I love y —"

Anakin tensed as her voice cut off. "Stay with me, Mom. Everything —"

He'd wanted to tell her that everything was going to be fine. And he wanted to tell her so much more. But before he could say anything, Shmi said again, "I love —" Then her eyes closed and her head fell back.

She died in his arms.

Anakin sat there in stunned silence, just holding his mother. *If I'd gotten here sooner, I could have saved her.* He pushed his fingers through Shmi's matted hair. *I won't leave her here. I have to get her back to the speeder bike. But those Tusken guards —*

He remembered the Tusken he'd encountered when he was a boy.

I saved his life!

Earlier, Anakin hadn't questioned the Tuskens' motives. Now, he wondered if they would have taken his mother if they'd known that her son had once saved one of their own. *Or is this how Tuskens say thank you?* He quickly speculated whether the Tusken he'd rescued might still be alive, possibly in this very camp. *I should have let him die! I should have!*

He thought of how the Tuskens had taken his mother, imagined what she had endured in the past month . . .

Why would they do this? How could anyone *do this?*

The answer came to him from the darkest reaches of his own heart. *They did this because they wanted to. They did this because they could.* As his grief transformed into anger, he knew exactly how he was going to dispose of the Tusken guards.

Temporarily leaving his mother's corpse, Anakin Skywalker stepped outside the tent and reactivated his lightsaber.

He didn't stop with the guards.

When Anakin arrived back at the Lars homestead with his mother's blanket-wrapped body, Cliegg Lars, Owen, Beru, Padmé, and C-3PO emerged from the entry dome. They watched in silence as he lifted his dead mother from the bike and carried her toward the dome's doorway. Anakin was in no mood to talk, and he had reconsidered his assessment that the Lars family was made up of "good people."

What's the advantage of being good if you're weak?

His grim, scowling expression locked onto Cliegg Lars, who lowered his gaze.

Perhaps you're wishing you hadn't given up on her so soon?

Without breaking stride, Anakin redirected his glare at Owen and Beru.

Maybe my mother never told you about how to be prepared to take care of things?

Anakin didn't even look at Padmé or the protocol droid as he descended with his mother into the underground dwelling.

Later, Anakin was standing at a workbench in the homestead garage, repairing a part from the swoop bike, when Padmé entered carrying a tray of food. She said, "I brought you something. Are you hungry?"

Anakin continued to examine the bike part, moving slowly, as if he was slightly dazed. "The shifter broke," he said. "Life seems so much simpler when you're fixing things. I'm good at fixing things. Always was. But I couldn't . . ." He stopped working and looked at Padmé. "Why'd she have to die? Why couldn't I save her? I know I *could* have." He turned away, looking into a dark corner of the cluttered garage. His rage had momentarily given way to grief.

"Sometimes there are things no one can fix," Padmé said. "You're not all-powerful, Ani."

"Well, I *should* be!" he snarled back at her, causing Padmé to flinch. "Someday I will be," he continued. "I will be the most powerful Jedi ever! I promise you. I will even learn to stop people from dying."

Padmé just stood there, confused and alarmed by his words. "Anakin . . ."

"It's all Obi-Wan's fault. He's jealous! He's holding me back!" He flung a wrench across the garage. It smashed against the wall and clattered to the floor.

"What's wrong, Ani?"

Still avoiding her gaze, Anakin tried to calm his voice as he said, "I . . . I killed them. I killed them all. They're dead. Every single one of them." He turned slowly to face Padmé, revealing the tears streaming down his face. "And not just the men, but the women and the children, too. They're like animals, and I slaughtered them like animals!" Then he roared, "I HATE them!"

Anakin began sobbing and slumped down to the floor. Padmé knelt and put her arms around him. She said, "To be angry is to be human."

"I'm a Jedi," Anakin gasped between sobs. "I know I'm better than this."

And yet he also knew something else, something far worse than that he'd allowed himself to give way to his anger.

Killing the Tuskens had given him satisfaction.

CHAPTER NINE

Anakin knelt before his mother's final resting place, a graveyard outside the Lars compound, where two old headstones stood beside the new one. "I wasn't strong enough to save you, Mom," he said, trying not to choke on his words. *I've failed*, he thought. *Not just as your son, but as a Jedi.* "I wasn't strong enough," he repeated. "But I promise I won't fail again." He rose to his feet. Through clenched teeth, he added, "I miss you so much."

Padmé, Cliegg, Owen, Beru, and C-3PO were gathered behind Anakin. As he moved away from the grave, R2-D2 motored toward the group and emitted a flurry of beeps and whistles.

"R2?" Padmé said, surprised that he had left their starship. "What are you doing here?"

R2-D2 beeped and whistled more.

Seizing the opportunity to act as a translator, C-3PO said, "It seems that he is carrying a message from an

Obi-Wan Kenobi. Hmm. Master Ani, does that name mean anything to you?"

The two droids followed Anakin and Padmé into the starship.

Obi-Wan had tracked the bounty hunter — a man named Jango Fett — to the droid foundries on the planet Geonosis, where he'd discovered that the Trade Federation's Viceroy, Nute Gunray, was behind the assassination attempts on Padmé. Obi-Wan had also learned that the Trade Federation was scheduled to take delivery of a Geonosian-produced droid army, and that various interstellar commerce factions had allied with Count Dooku's Separatist movement. Although Obi-Wan had managed to transmit this information from Geonosis, his holographic recording ended with him trying to evade a hail of laserfire from enemy droids.

Anakin and Padmé watched the prerecorded message in their starship's cockpit on Tatooine, while the Jedi Council and Chancellor Palpatine simultaneously viewed the relayed transmission on Coruscant. When Obi-Wan's message was over, Jedi Master Mace Windu instructed Anakin to stay where he was with Senator Amidala while the Jedi Council dealt with Count Dooku. "Protect the Senator at all costs," Mace Windu said via holographic transmission. "That is your first priority."

"Understood, Master," Anakin replied. *First I lose my mother, now . . . Obi-Wan.*

As Mace Windu's hologram faded out, Padmé said, "They'll never get there in time to save him. They have to come halfway across the galaxy." Swiveling in her seat to examine coordinates on the navicomputer console, she said, "Look, Geonosis is less than a parsec away."

"If he's still alive," Anakin said grimly.

"Ani, are you just going to sit here and let him die? He's your friend, your mentor. He's —"

"He's like my father!" Anakin snapped. *The father I never had.* "But you heard Master Windu. He gave me strict orders to stay here."

"He gave you strict orders to protect me," Padmé said as she flicked a series of switches that activated the ship's engines, "and I'm going to help Obi-Wan. If you plan to protect me, you will have to come along."

Anakin grinned.

As the ship lifted off, carrying Anakin, Padmé, and the two droids away from Tatooine, it occurred to Anakin that they hadn't so much as said good-bye to Clieg, Owen, or Beru. *I didn't have much to say to them anyway*, he thought. He looked at C-3PO, who had belted his sandblasted metal body into a seat behind Anakin, and felt some small sense of accomplishment.

At least I rescued someone *I cared about from Tatooine.*

Although Obi-Wan Kenobi turned out to be very much alive, Anakin's unauthorized mission to Geonosis was almost a disaster. He and Padmé were captured by the insectoid Geonosians before they could rescue Obi-Wan, and then the duplicitous Count Dooku and the Geonosians sentenced them to death.

And yet to Anakin, all of this amounted to *almost* a disaster, because there had been one bright, significant moment on Geonosis for him and Padmé. After they had been captured and enchained, and were about to be hauled into a giant execution arena, Padmé had faced him and said, "I'm not afraid to die. I've been dying a little bit each day since you came back into my life."

Dying? "What are you talking about?" Anakin asked.

"I love you."

"You love me?" Anakin said incredulously. "I thought that we had decided not to fall in love, that we would be forced to live a lie, and that it would destroy our lives."

"I think our lives are about to be destroyed anyway," Padmé said sadly. "I truly, deeply love you, and before we die I want you to know."

They kissed then, and at that moment, Anakin believed he had more reason to live than ever before.

Anakin, Padmé, and Obi-Wan were nearly killed by monsters in a giant execution arena. Fortunately, their deaths were prevented by the arrival of lightsaber-wielding Jedi, including Mace Windu and Yoda, and an unexpected army of clone soldiers. Although Mace Windu was able to dispose of Jango Fett, who had served as the genetic template for the clones, many Jedi perished in the battle against the Geonosian-manufactured droids.

Count Dooku fled the execution arena, and Obi-Wan and Anakin chased him to an abandoned weapons factory in a high rock tower that Dooku had converted into a hangar for his personal starship, a customized solar sailer. With their lightsabers already activated, Obi-Wan and Anakin entered the dark hangar to find the elegantly attired, silver-haired former Jedi as he prepared to escape from Geonosis. Turning to face his pursuers, Dooku wore an expression of mild annoyance at the pair who now stood across the hangar from him.

Even though Dooku had renounced the Jedi order ten years earlier, Anakin noticed that the man had a curved-handled lightsaber clipped to his belt. Anakin snarled, "You're gonna pay for all the Jedi that you killed today, Dooku."

Knowing Dooku's reputation as a swordsman, Obi-Wan kept his eyes on Dooku as he stepped closer to Anakin and said in a low voice, "We'll take him together. Go in slowly on the left."

But Anakin was all out of patience. "I'm taking him now!" he shouted as he ignored Obi-Wan's protests and charged Dooku. He was barely halfway across the hangar's mosaic floor when Dooku, instead of reaching for his lightsaber, raised and aimed his right hand in Anakin's direction.

Anakin screamed and involuntarily squeezed his eyes shut as brilliant blue bolts of lightning suddenly enveloped his body. Overwhelmed by the intense pain, he could not even begin to think how Dooku was controlling and directing the lightning at him. Anakin felt his feet leave the floor, and then he was hurled across the chamber and smashed into the wall. He screamed again as he landed on the hard floor, still feeling the surge of dark energy that Dooku had unleashed upon him. His body felt as if it had been seared, and as he writhed on the floor, he realized smoke was rising from his tunic.

He struggled to stay conscious. Trying to block out the pain, he was only peripherally aware that Obi-Wan had engaged Dooku in a lightsaber fight. *I should have listened to Obi-Wan!* He thought of Padmé. *I can't die like this!*

As Anakin lay on the floor and struggled to recover, he attempted to open his eyes and felt more agony. It was as if the electric shock was still licking at his eyeballs. For a moment, he wondered if he had been blinded by the lightning.

Have to focus! He concentrated, tried to get his breathing under control. A moment later, his vision returned, allowing him to watch helplessly as Dooku's red-bladed lightsaber slashed at Obi-Wan's left arm and leg. Obi-Wan dropped his lightsaber as he collapsed to the floor.

Smoke was still rising from Anakin's clothes. He watched with mounting horror as Dooku raised his lightsaber and prepared to bring it down on the helpless Obi-Wan.

Finding some unexpected reserve from within himself, Anakin roared as he ignited his lightsaber and leapt across the hangar to block Dooku's death blow. While Obi-Wan's limp form lay beneath the crossed lightsabers, Dooku eyed Anakin and said, "Brave of you, boy. But I would have thought you had learned your lesson."

"I am a slow learner," Anakin said as he maneuvered Dooku away from Obi-Wan's form.

"Anakin!" Obi-Wan shouted. He'd used the Force to retrieve his fallen lightsaber, and managed to toss it to his Padawan. Anakin caught and activated it so that he was now using two lightsabers against his opponent. But only several swift contacts later, Dooku's blade swept through Obi-Wan's weapon, shattering the handle and nearly severing Anakin's fingertips. Anakin still clutched his own weapon in his other hand, and the duel continued across the hangar.

Trying to suppress his anger, Anakin reached out to the Force as his eyes locked on Dooku's. Their lightsabers blurred at the edges of his vision, and he believed the Force would guide him to defeat Dooku. But as he continued to meet Dooku's condescending stare, he felt his rage begin to rise again.

And then Dooku made his move, sweeping his blade through Anakin's sword arm, just above the elbow. Anakin shouted and felt his breath go out of him as Dooku used the Force to launch him backward through the air. Then everything went dark.

Anakin didn't know how many minutes had passed as he began to return to consciousness. He felt something shift behind his head, and realized he was lying against Obi-Wan's legs. Obi-Wan pushed himself up from the hangar floor, then helped Anakin rise. Anakin saw Yoda standing in the middle of the hangar. Parts of the ceiling had broken away, and there was rubble all over the floor.

What happened?

Then Anakin noticed Dooku's solar sailer was gone.

"Anakin!" Padmé shouted. She had arrived at the hangar with a squad of clone troopers, and it hurt him to see her anguished expression as she came running toward him, seeing what was left of his right arm. She wrapped her arms carefully around him.

At least you're safe, he thought, wrapping his left arm around her to hold her close. He didn't care that Obi-Wan or Yoda were watching. He was dazed and maimed, and he was afraid if he let go of Padmé, his knees would buckle and he'd pass out again. And so he just stood there, holding her.

In the end, not even Master Yoda had been able to prevent Dooku from fleeing into space, or stop the worlds of the Republic from entering a civil war. The Clone Wars had begun.

To make matters worse, Count Dooku had told Obi-Wan that hundreds of Senators were under the control of a Sith Lord called Darth Sidious. Although the Jedi did not consider Dooku a trustworthy source, they agreed to keep a closer eye on the Senate.

Following his duel with Dooku, Anakin was outfitted with a cybernetic arm, and he escorted Padmé back to Naboo. There, on the same terrace by the lake where they had exchanged their first tentative kiss, they arranged a secret meeting with a Naboo holy man. Padmé was dressed in a white gown with flowered trim and Anakin wore his formal Jedi robes. With C-3PO and R2-D2 as their only witnesses, they were married.

Anakin had no idea how long they could keep their marriage a secret, but he didn't care. *She's mine. At last, my beloved Padmé is mine.* It was truly a dream come true. And on their wedding day, it was easy for him to believe that his greatest troubles were behind him.

He never imagined the nightmares that were yet to come.

CHAPTER TEN

Almost overnight, the Galactic Republic acquired a massive military force that included interstellar battleships, weapon-laden starfighters, and enormous ground vehicles. While Senators argued whether Supreme Chancellor Palpatine had been wrong to conscript and deploy the hastily raised Grand Army of the Republic, more worlds were quick to join Count Dooku's Separatist movement, which had officially named itself the Confederacy of Independent Systems. As Master Yoda had foreseen, the Clone Wars spread like an explosive virus throughout the galaxy.

Although Palpatine had always presented himself as a cautious, unassuming politician, he made it known to all that he would do whatever was necessary to preserve the Republic. Despite his modest protests, the Senate demanded that he stay in office long after his term had expired. But as the Clone Wars escalated, even his most trusted advisors were surprised by his many amendments to the Republic Constitution, which extended his own political powers while limiting the freedom of others.

The Jedi Council reluctantly agreed to allow Jedi to serve as generals to the Grand Army's clone troops. However, not every Jedi was willing to engage in warfare; some chose to serve as healers, and others abandoned the Jedi order entirely.

Compelled to fight on behalf of the Republic, Obi-Wan Kenobi became a general, and Anakin, like many other Padawans, was promoted to knighthood sooner than expected to accommodate the Grand Army's needs. Although members of the Jedi Council observed that Anakin was still prone to arrogance and impatience, no one disputed the fact that he continued to grow even stronger with the power of the Force.

Lethal droids were not the only adversaries to the Jedi, as Count Dooku had recruited such deadly beings as the Sith aspirant Asajj Ventress and the nearly indestructible Gen'Dai bounty hunter, Durge, to fight on his behalf. Dooku himself had trained Ventress in the art of lightsaber combat, but often ridiculed her preference to wield two lightsabers at the same time. Anakin nearly defeated Ventress on the fourth moon of the gas giant Yavin. One of their duels, in the industrial sector of Coruscant, left him with a deep scar on the right side of his face.

Three years after the Battle of Geonosis, Ventress and Durge no longer posed a threat, but Count Dooku led the Confederacy, and the Jedi were no closer to finding the mysterious Darth Sidious. The Clone Wars raged on.

After destroying a secret Confederacy laboratory on the planet Nelvaan in the Outer Rim, Anakin and Obi-Wan were leaving with R2-D2 in a Republic Star Destroyer when they received an urgent message. R2-D2 plugged into a communications console and projected a hologram of Mace Windu, who said, "Kenobi, Skywalker. Coruscant is under siege, and General Grievous has abducted the Supreme Chancellor. You must return immediately. You must rescue Palpatine."

"Grievous," Anakin snarled as the holographic message ended. Count Dooku's most notorious lieutenant, the cyborg General Grievous commanded the Confederacy's droid armies. Grievous had been trained in lightsaber combat by Dooku himself, and had a penchant for killing Jedi and collecting their lightsabers. Although some Jedi wondered just how much Palpatine was trying to end the war, Anakin had come to consider the Republic's leader among his most trusted friends.

I won't let the Chancellor die! Anakin vowed to himself.

Stepping away from R2-D2 and Obi-Wan, Anakin addressed the armored clone troops in the Star Destroyer's hangar. "Battle stations. All crews to their fighters. Prepare to jump into hyperspace. Move!"

Republic Star Destroyers and Confederacy gunships were fully engaged in an explosive battle over the skies of Coruscant when Anakin and Obi-Wan returned from the Outer Rim. Antifighter flak flashed in bright bursts near every ship, and decimated vessels tumbled from orbit and smashed into the spires of the city-covered world below.

Flanked by a squadron of veteran clone aviators and with R2-D2 acting as Anakin's copilot, the two Jedi left their own Star Destroyer in a pair of starfighters and raced into the melee. Blasting droid ships while evading missiles, Anakin and Obi-Wan courageously made their way through the deadly flow of enemy vessels until they infiltrated the Confederate flagship, *Invisible Hand*, on which Supreme Chancellor Palpatine was held hostage by General Grievous.

To increase speed and maneuverability, Jedi starfighters were engineered without shield generators. Although this led some opponents to believe that such starfighters were more vulnerable to attack, most Jedi pilots were adept at using the Force to anticipate, evade, and attack their enemies. Anakin was considered among the top pilots in the Jedi order, but unlike other Jedi, he did not hesitate to rely upon technology to help achieve his goals. The way Anakin saw things, the Force had not been enough to save his own right arm or stop Dooku on Geonosis, and he doubted the war would be won by the Force alone either.

The Jedi moved stealthily through the ship until they reached the *Invisible Hand*'s main communications and sensors pod, a lofty chamber with expansive windows that provided a 180-degree view of the surrounding space battle. It was in this chamber that they found Supreme Chancellor Palpatine, who sat in a tall chair, his wrists pinned by energy binders to the chair's arms. Palpatine's face was pale, and he did not look relieved to see the Jedi.

"Are you all right?" Anakin asked as he and Obi-Wan approached the Chancellor's seated form.

Palpatine nervously looked past the two Jedi and said, "Count Dooku."

Anakin and Obi-Wan turned and looked up to see the impeccably attired Dooku and two super battle droids step onto an elevated balcony that hugged the aft wall of the chamber. Although Dooku was in his ninth decade, he moved with the grace of a jungle predator. Anakin's mind flashed back to his confrontation with Dooku on Geonosis, when he'd made the mistake of charging Dooku without Obi-Wan right at his side.

Keeping his eyes on Dooku as he addressed Anakin, Obi-Wan said, "This time we will do it together."

"I was about to say that," Anakin said.

Dooku stepped away from his droids, leapt over the balcony's railing, and executed a neat flip before landing a short distance from the Jedi. He reached to his side and drew his lightsaber.

"Get help," Palpatine said urgently from his seat. "You're no match for him. He's a Sith Lord."

Obi-Wan offered an assuring smile. "Chancellor Palpatine, Sith Lords are our specialty." Obi-Wan and Anakin shed their Jedi robes, letting them fall to the floor as they drew their own lightsabers.

"Your swords, please," Dooku urged as he walked toward the Jedi. "We don't want to make a mess of things in front of the Chancellor."

"You won't get away this time, Dooku," Obi-Wan said. He and Obi-Wan ignited their blue-bladed light-sabers and advanced on Dooku, who ignited his own red-bladed weapon. The beams of their lightsabers hummed and clashed as they moved across the chamber. Dooku defended himself effortlessly.

On the level above, the two droids didn't budge, but watched silently as the figures came to a momentary standstill. While the three lightsabers continued to blaze, Dooku grinned at his opponents and said, "I've been looking forward to this."

Not intimidated by the elder swordsman, Anakin said, "My powers have doubled since the last time we met, Count."

"Good," Dooku said. "Twice the pride, double the fall."

The Jedi charged once again. Dooku backed up as he parried their blows, then used the Force to throw Obi-Wan to the floor. As Anakin continued his assault on Dooku, forcing him back up the steps to the upper level, Obi-Wan recovered himself and leapt up to rejoin the fight.

The two droids fired at Obi-Wan, but he batted their fired energy bolts back at them and cut them down as he moved fast for Dooku. Unfortunately, Dooku moved faster, extending his left hand toward Obi-Wan as he used the Force to lift the Jedi off his feet while at the same time constricting his throat. As Obi-Wan gasped, Anakin swung at Dooku from behind, but Dooku kicked Anakin's stomach with his left foot, smashing the young Jedi against a nearby wall.

Obi-Wan was still suspended in the air when Dooku gestured again with his hand to send his choking victim sailing across the chamber. Obi-Wan crashed against the railing of an extended balcony, then collapsed like a broken doll to the floor. With another gesture, Dooku used the Force to tear a section of the balcony away from its braces and pin Obi-Wan's unconscious form to the floor.

Master!

Anakin threw himself at Dooku, knocking him from the balcony to the floor below. Leaping down after his quarry, Anakin struck again and again at Dooku until both of their blades were practically locked onto each other.

"I sense great fear in you, Skywalker," Dooku said. "You have hate. You have anger. But you don't use them."

Anakin grimaced, angrier than before, the blades unlocked, and the duel resumed. Trading blows across the chamber, they came to a stop near the hostage Palpatine. Dooku was using both hands to grip his lightsaber, putting more of his strength into each deadly swing, when Anakin reached out fast with his left hand to catch Dooku's wrists. In the moment that Dooku was temporarily pinned, Anakin's right hand twisted sharply to swing his lightsaber between him and the startled Dooku.

Dooku's lightsaber automatically deactivated as it flew out of his severed hands, which fell to the floor with an ugly flopping sound. His knees buckled, and he dropped to kneel beside his hands. Anakin snatched Dooku's lightsaber from the air, then activated the red blade and crossed it with the blade of his own weapon, angling the blades to either side of his opponent's head. Dooku's eyes were wide and his mouth agape as he stared at the maimed ends of his arms. Because lightsabers cauterize as fast as they cleave through flesh, there was surprisingly little blood.

I got you, Anakin thought, keeping the lightsaber blades close to Dooku's neck.

"Good, Anakin," Palpatine said from his seat. "Good." Unexpectedly, he chuckled.

He almost sounds cheerful. He must be in shock.

Then Palpatine said, "Kill him."

What? Anakin kept his eyes on Dooku, who shifted his trembling gaze to Palpatine.

"Kill him now," Palpatine said.

Dooku looked up at Anakin, who now saw genuine fear in the old, maimed man's eyes. Anakin said, "I shouldn't." His words seemed to give some relief to Dooku, whose panicked expression relaxed slightly as he continued to tremble. *I can be merciful*, Anakin thought as he held Dooku's gaze. *I'm a better Jedi than you ever were.*

"Do it," Palpatine said, practically spitting the words out.

Fear flickered again in Dooku's eyes, as he suddenly sensed what was coming.

Anakin rapidly uncrossed the blades, cleaving through Dooku's neck. Dooku's body collapsed alongside his hands, while his head rolled and thudded across the floor like an ill-shaped ball. Anakin felt his own heart pounding in his chest as he deactivated the lightsabers, and almost immediately thought, *What have I done?*

"You did well, Anakin," Palpatine said calmly. "He was too dangerous to be kept alive."

"Yes, but he was an unarmed prisoner," Anakin said

as he released Palpatine's energy binders. "I shouldn't have done that. It's not the Jedi way."

Rising from the tall seat, Palpatine said, "It is only natural. He cut off your arm, and you wanted revenge. It wasn't the first time, Anakin. Remember what you told me about your mother and the Sand People?"

In the three years since his mother's death, Anakin had convinced himself that he had temporarily lost his mind that night at the Tusken camp. It remained his darkest secret, something he'd never even told Obi-Wan because he knew he would be banished from the Jedi order, and yet he'd felt compelled to take Palpatine into his confidence. Anakin grimaced at the memory of the slaughtered Tuskens. The desire to kill them had been beyond his control. *Killing Dooku wasn't the same. I knew it was wrong, but I did it anyway.*

Palpatine said, "Now we must leave before more security droids arrive."

Anakin ran to Obi-Wan, who remained pinned under the broken section of the balcony. Outside the chamber's large windows a ripple of fiery bursts indicated the space battle had intensified.

"Anakin, there's no time," Palpatine said as Anakin pulled his Master free from the wreckage. "We must get off this ship before it's too late." The *Invisible Hand* shuddered violently as it was wracked by a series of explosions.

Checking Obi-Wan's vital signs, Anakin said, "He seems to be all right."

"Leave him," Palpatine commanded, "or we'll never make it."

"His fate will be the same as ours," Anakin said, for once refusing to obey the Chancellor. He lifted and slung Obi-Wan's body over his shoulders and ran with Palpatine to the lift tube.

Anakin and Palpatine were still aboard the *Invisible Hand* when Obi-Wan recovered. Along with R2-D2, they were briefly apprehended by General Grievous but managed to evade his metallic clutches. Unfortunately, Grievous launched all the escape pods and fled into space as the battle-damaged *Invisible Hand* began to tumble through Coruscant's upper atmosphere. Although the crash landing was bone-jarring for Palpatine and the Jedi, Anakin's incredible piloting skills delivered them, and what little remained of the Confederate flagship, to a landing strip.

Mace Windu, Senator Bail Organa of Alderaan, and C-3PO were among the dignitaries who greeted Palpatine and Anakin at the Chancellor's private landing platform at the Senate Offices while Obi-Wan returned to the Jedi Temple. After speaking briefly with Bail Organa as they entered the office building, Anakin found Padmé discreetly waiting for him in the shadows of a tall column. He hadn't seen her in months.

Although Anakin was concerned that General Grievous was still at large and had assumed leadership of the Confederacy, he forgot his troubles as he embraced Padmé.

But she seemed different; she had something very important to tell him.

CHAPTER ELEVEN

"Ani, I'm pregnant."

Still in the shadows of the Senate Offices hall-way, Anakin suddenly felt light-headed. Padmé stared into his eyes, waiting for him to say something. "That's —" he began, then sighed and looked away. With the sudden realization that their marriage could not be a secret much longer, his first thoughts were of how this development would impact on their lives. *Padmé might be recalled to Naboo, and I'll be cast out in disgrace from the Jedi order. It will be a scandal. . . .*

Then his gaze met Padmé's again, and he saw how frightened she was.

"Well," he said, "that's won — that's wonderful!" He smiled.

Less than assured, Padmé said, "What are we going to do?"

"We're not going to worry about anything right now," Anakin said, holding her tight. "All right? This is a happy moment. The happiest moment of my life."

Later that night, in Padmé's apartment in Galactic City, Anakin had a nightmare so terrible that he nearly shouted when he awoke. He tried to ease himself out of bed quietly so Padmé would not be aware of his absence, but she woke up too and found him standing on the terrace, watching the air traffic glide past her apartment windows.

"What's bothering you?" Padmé asked.

"Nothing," he said. Padmé was wearing the good-luck charm that Anakin had carved for her shortly after they'd met. He reached out to touch the charm and said, "I remember when I gave this to you."

Padmé gave him a hard stare and said, "How long is it going to take us to be honest with each other?"

Anakin took a deep breath. "It was a dream," he admitted.

"Bad?"

"Like the ones I used to have about my mother . . . just before she died."

"And?"

"And it was about you."

Padmé moved closer to Anakin and said, "Tell me."

Anakin moved a short distance away. "It was only a dream," he said, but as soon as the words had been uttered, he felt them to be untrue.

It wasn't just a dream. It was real, and it's going to happen.

He turned to face Padmé and said, "You die in childbirth."

Padmé tried not to cringe. "And the baby?"

"I don't know."

Padmé moved again to Anakin's side. "It was only a dream," she said, now trying to convince herself as well as placate Anakin.

"I won't let this one become real," Anakin vowed.

"This baby will change our lives," Padmé said. "I doubt the queen will continue to allow me to serve in the Senate. And if the Council discovers you're the father, you'll be expelled."

"I — I know," Anakin stammered, trying to push away those realities. "I know."

"Do you think Obi-Wan might be able to help us?"

"We don't need his help," Anakin said, and glowered as he imagined his Master's reprimands. When he noticed that Padmé looked frightened by his expression, Anakin shifted his features into a gentle smile and said, "Our baby is a blessing."

Anakin thought about the dream again, hoping that it wasn't an accurate depiction of things to come, but somehow knowing in his heart that it was. Fortunately, he knew someone who was something of an expert on premonitions.

"Premonitions?" Master Yoda said. "Premonitions. Hmm."

It was the morning after his nightmare about Padmé, and Anakin was in Yoda's quarters in the Jedi Temple. They were seated across from each other, and shafts of bright sunlight sifted through the blinds that lined the windows of the sparsely furnished room.

Yoda said, "These visions you have —"

"They're of pain, suffering. Death."

"Yourself you speak of, or someone you know?"

Anakin was reluctant to offer too many details, but admitted, "Someone."

"Close to you?"

Anakin lowered his gaze, and felt almost ashamed as he answered, "Yes."

Raising a cautionary finger, Yoda fixed Anakin with a penetrating gaze and said, "Careful you must be when sensing the future, Anakin. The fear of loss is a path to the dark side."

Anakin recalled the dreams that had preceded his mother's death, and then of his failure to save her. Returning Yoda's gaze, he said flatly, "I won't let these visions come true, Master Yoda."

"Death is a natural part of life," Yoda explained. "Rejoice for those around you who transform into the Force. Mourn them, do not. Miss them, do not. Attachment leads to jealousy. The shadow of greed that is."

Hoping to stay on the right path this time, Anakin said, "What must I do, Master Yoda?"

"Train yourself to let go of everything you fear to lose."

I might be able to let go of being a Jedi, Anakin thought, *but I can't let go of Padmé. I just can't. I love her too much.*

I won't let her die. I won't.

Soon after Anakin's meeting with Yoda, Palpatine confided to Anakin that he feared the Jedi Council wanted more control than they already had in the Republic. Anakin found this difficult to believe, but agreed to become Palpatine's personal representative on the Council. Because only Jedi Masters served on the Council, Anakin assumed that his appointment would guarantee his promotion to Master, and felt insulted when the Council insisted that he remain a Knight. After his first awkward meeting with the Council, Anakin learned from Obi-Wan that the Council wanted him to report on all of Chancellor Palpatine's dealings. It seemed that Anakin was the *only* Jedi who trusted Palpatine.

Palpatine suspects the Council is up to something, and the Council wants me to spy on Palpatine! Who should I trust? Anakin tried talking with Padmé, but when she expressed her concern that democracy no longer existed in the Republic, he accused her of sounding like a Separatist. *Is she turning against me too?!*

Later that night, Palpatine summoned Anakin to meet him in the Chancellor's private box at the Galaxies Opera House. There, while watching a troupe of Mon Calamari perform a zero-gravity ballet within immense spheres of shimmering water, Palpatine informed Anakin that Clone Intelligence Units had discovered that General Grievous was hiding in the Utapau system. After dismissing his aides from the box, Palpatine further confided that he had come to suspect that the Jedi Council wanted to control the Republic, and was plotting to betray him.

Palpatine said, "They asked you to spy on me, didn't they?"

Squirming in his seat beside the Chancellor, Anakin replied, "I don't, uh . . . I don't know what to say."

"Remember back to your early teachings," Palpatine continued. "All those who gain power are afraid to lose it. Even the Jedi."

No, that's not true, Anakin thought. "The Jedi use their power for good," he insisted.

"Good is a point of view, Anakin," Palpatine said calmly. "The Sith and the Jedi are similar in almost every way, including their quest for greater power."

That's not true, either. "The Sith rely on their passion

for their strength," Anakin said. "They think inwards, only about themselves."

"And the Jedi don't?" Palpatine asked, lifting his eyebrows high to convey his belief that the answer was as plain as his face.

"The Jedi are selfless," Anakin countered. "They only care about others."

There was applause from the audience, and Anakin and Palpatine directed their attention to the performers. Palpatine said, "Did you ever hear the tragedy of Darth Plagueis the Wise?"

"No," Anakin admitted.

"I thought not," Palpatine said smugly. "It's not a story the Jedi would tell you. It's a Sith legend. Darth Plagueis was a Dark Lord of the Sith, so powerful and so wise he could use the Force to influence the midichlorians to create . . . life." He slowly turned his gaze to Anakin before he continued. "He had such a knowledge of the dark side that he could even keep the ones he cared about from dying."

Anakin thought immediately of Padmé, and of his most recent nightmares, and felt a tingling sensation along his spine. He said, "He could actually . . . save people from death?"

"The dark side of the Force is a pathway to many abilities some consider to be *unnatural*."

Anakin thought about Darth Plagueis, wondering

just how much of the legend might be true. He said, "Wh — What happened to him?"

Looking away from Anakin, Palpatine answered slowly, "He became so powerful, the only thing he was afraid of was losing his power, which eventually, of course, he did. Unfortunately, he taught his apprentice everything he knew. Then his apprentice killed him in his sleep. It's ironic. He could save others from death, but not himself."

Because the Chancellor was such a learned man and had discussed the ongoing hunt for Darth Sidious with members of the Jedi Council, Anakin wasn't curious about how he might have learned such a bizarre story about the Sith. Anakin only wanted to know one thing.

"Is it possible to learn this power?" he asked.

Raising his eyebrows, Palpatine turned to once again lock his gaze on Anakin and said, "Not from a Jedi."

Twenty-three years after the end of the Clone Wars, Darth Vader had no difficulty recalling Anakin Skywalker's meeting with Supreme Chancellor Palpatine at the Opera House. Although he had not yet realized that Palpatine was really the Sith Lord Darth Sidious, it was at that particular moment that Anakin Skywalker decided he must learn the secrets of the Sith.

At the time, Anakin had convinced himself that he only wanted to gain the powers that would help him save his wife. He hadn't wanted to take the path to the dark side. In fact, he had continued to behave nobly after that meeting at the opera. When the Jedi Council insulted him yet again by selecting Obi-Wan to hunt down General Grievous on Utapau, Anakin apologized for his arrogance. And after he learned that Palpatine was the Sith Lord who had slain Darth Plagueis, and realized that the Chancellor had no intention of stepping down from his position of power after the death of

General Grievous, Anakin reported his discovery to Mace Windu, who led a team of Jedi Masters to apprehend Palpatine. Anakin had done the right thing.

But because Anakin believed that the only way he could save Padmé was by gaining Palpatine's arcane knowledge, he had been unable to let Mace Windu kill the Sith Lord. And so he had allowed Palpatine to unleash Sith Lightning on Mace Windu, and chose to betray all the Jedi on Coruscant, and pledged himself to Palpatine.

As the Sith Lord's new apprentice, he had taken the name Darth Vader before he set out to kill every Jedi who remained at the Jedi Temple. Now, so many years later, Vader reflected on all the Jedi he killed that day. Remembering the stunned expressions of Mace Windu as he fell from Palpatine's office window and the screams of the Jedi younglings and their teachers, he felt no remorse. Just as he believed he had done his best to be a dutiful Jedi, he believed his actions as Palpatine's apprentice were even more righteous.

Smoke had been still billowing from the Jedi Temple when Vader traveled to the volcanic world of Mustafar to kill the Separatist leaders in their hideout. Meanwhile, Palpatine initiated an order for all off-world clone troops to kill their Jedi generals, and then informed the Senate that the Separatists had been defeated and the Jedi rebellion had been foiled. Joyous cheers had accompanied Palpatine's declaration that the Republic would be reorganized into the first Galactic Empire.

After killing all the Separatist leaders, Palpatine's new apprentice had stepped outside the mountain fortress on Mustafar to gaze at the blazing lava rivers below. He would not mourn for the lives he had taken. But for the loss of his former self, the boy who had dreamed of becoming a Jedi, he was unable to hold back the tears that streamed down his cheeks.

Anakin Skywalker was gone. Or was he? After all, Padmé had fallen in love with Anakin, not Darth Vader.

He had not anticipated that Padmé, traveling with C-3PO, would follow him to Mustafar and refute the righteousness of his actions. Nor had he foreseen that Obi-Wan would survive the Jedi purge, and that the deceitful Padmé would bring him with her. Despite his powers and years of attunement to Obi-Wan, his rage had blocked his ability to sense his former Master's presence on Mustafar until he saw the Jedi standing in the hatch of Padmé's starship.

He also never imagined that Obi-Wan possessed the strength to bring him down so brutally.

CHAPTER TWELVE

"You were the Chosen One!" Obi-Wan shouted down at what was left of Anakin Skywalker, who writhed at the bottom of a slope of black sand at the edge of a lava river on Mustafar. Their exhausting duel had carried them far from the landing pad where Padmé's ship had arrived, and where Anakin had used the Force to choke his seemingly treacherous wife.

But now the duel was over. With a single sweep of his lightsaber, Obi-Wan had severed his former Padawan's legs at the knees and also his left arm.

As Anakin struggled to raise his head from the smoldering sand, his eyes blazed with fury as he glared at Obi-Wan. *I won't die like this! I'm still stronger than you!*

"It was said you would destroy the Sith, not join them!" Obi-Wan continued. "Bring balance to the Force, not leave it in darkness!"

Feeling the intense heat permeating his torn tunic,

Anakin sighted his fallen lightsaber lying a short distance away. Too stunned and dazed to focus his powers, he watched with rage as Obi-Wan bent down to pick up the lightsaber, then took it with him as he began walking up the slope.

"I hate you!" Anakin roared, keeping his eyes focused on the departing figure.

Obi-Wan stopped in his tracks and turned one final time to face the ruined, seething monster. "You were my brother, Anakin," Obi-Wan said. "I loved you."

Anakin's clothes caught fire, and he was suddenly engulfed in flames. His screams were filled with anger as well as pain, not unlike that of any entirely helpless creature. His instinct was to roll and put out the flames, but because of his wounds and the red-hot stones beneath his ravaged head and torso, all he could do was burn and burn.

Obi-Wan walked off, leaving Anakin to die. Somehow, through his agony, Anakin felt one last flicker of Obi-Wan's presence before the Jedi receded from view.

Anakin kept screaming.

The flames finally burned out.

Anakin's mechanical right arm dug into the sand.

He pulled, and slid a few millimeters up the slope.

Again!

With each movement, hot volcanic shards scraped and tore at his roasted flesh. It took all of his concentration to shift his scorched remains up the slope and away from the lava river.

He moaned. Only his powers kept him from blacking out.

Again!

Only his hatred for Obi-Wan made him want to live another day.

Anakin — he still thought of himself as Anakin — heard the engine of an arriving starship travel over his position. He had no idea how much time had passed before he heard a clone trooper's voice call out, "Your majesty, this way."

Then he heard Palpatine's voice, "There he is. He's still alive."

Anakin's blackened torso went completely limp as he finally allowed darkness to sweep over him.

Anakin awoke on an operating table, surrounded by droids. The recently appointed Emperor Palpatine had brought him to a surgical reconstruction center on Coruscant, and the droids were busily attaching robotic limbs to his quivering torso, which was strapped to the table by strong metal belts. The droids were working fast to maintain the precious midi-chlorians that existed in Anakin's blood and tissue. To prevent the midi-chlorians from becoming thinned by intrusive chemicals, the droids were working without anesthetics.

Anakin felt everything.

He felt each cold metal blade that sliced into his hideously scarred flesh to allow more tools to probe and stabilize his damaged internal organs. He squirmed as shattered bones were replaced by plastoid, and cringed as lasers grafted the new limbs into place. At some point, he overheard a surgical droid explaining to Palpatine that he would require a special helmet and backpack to cycle air in and out of his damaged lungs.

Despite this damage, throughout the entire procedure, he never stopped screaming.

Finally stabilized, Anakin lay quietly on the table to which he was still secured. He was clad in a gleaming black life-support suit with a lighted control function panel set across his chest. He watched as a robot mechanism above his head slowly lowered a black mask with oval vision receptors and a triangular respiratory vent over his face, while another mechanism placed a helmet over his skull. The helmet and mask locked onto each other as they simultaneously bolted to the armored ring that wrapped around his neck. Fully encased within the pressurized suit, he heard a labored, mechanical rasp, then realized it was the sound of his own breathing.

The table tilted, raising Anakin's restrained body to a standing position. From the shadows of the operating room, the hooded Emperor stepped forward and said, "Lord Vader. Can you hear me?"

Vader? That's right . . . I'm Darth Vader. Anakin is gone.

Vader exhaled, then said, "Yes, Master." The mask's vocabulator had transformed his voice into a commanding baritone. He still felt weak, so it was with some difficulty that he slowly turned his head, adjusting his vision through the helmet to better see the Emperor. The Emperor's face was gnarled and twisted, deformed by the Sith lightning that had been briefly deflected by Mace Windu during their battle.

"Where is Padmé?" Vader said in his new voice. After everything that had happened, he was still concerned for her, still loved her, still wanted to save her life. "Is she safe? Is she all right?"

In his most sympathetic tone, Palpatine said, "It seems, in your anger, you killed her."

"I? I couldn't have," Vader said with disbelief. *I loved her! I did everything I could to save* — his mind's voice sounded strange to him, weaker than the synthesized roll of thunder that emitted from his mask. He recalled choking Padmé on Mustafar, watching her body crumple and fall on the landing pad.

I didn't mean to —

Vader snarled, "She was alive. I felt it!"

Palpatine took a cautious step backward as Vader moaned with grief and rage. Around the laboratory, equipment and droids began to rupture and burst as

Vader lashed out in all directions with his Force powers. There was a loud snap of metal as he tore his left arm free from the table, then his right. He lurched forward on alloy legs that were fitted into cumbersome boots until he stood at the edge of the surgical floor. And somehow, through all his anger, he suddenly sensed at least one truth: Padmé was dead, along with their unborn child.

"No!" he bellowed so loud and long that his cry echoed off the walls. Behind his mask, he squeezed his eyes shut in an effort to hold back the tears that he was physically unable to wipe away.

But no tears came. He didn't know whether the surgical droids had altered or removed his tear ducts, and he was beyond caring. All he knew for certain was that Padmé was gone from him forever . . . and that there were more than a few Jedi still waiting to be killed.

Devoid of love for anyone, and unable to feel the touch of anything through his gloved, cybernetic fingers, Darth Vader was finally ready to fully embrace the dark side.

And so he did.

CHAPTER THIRTEEN

Darth Vader's earliest missions involved tracking down the Jedi who had survived the purge. He investigated every reported sighting, traveled to many remote worlds to hunt his quarry, and killed every Jedi he found. No reports led to Obi-Wan or Yoda, but Vader remained ever vigilant.

With every passing day, Vader distanced himself from the Jedi he had been. Where Anakin Skywalker had been influenced by traumatic circumstances, Vader shaped himself by inflicting pain on others. Unfortunately, because of his artificial arms, he was unable to conjure Sith Lightning or be invulnerable to it. He would always be weaker than the Emperor.

Few people were aware of what had become of Anakin Skywalker, but it was not long before nearly everyone in the Galactic Empire had heard some rumor or stray fact about Palpatine's new servant. One month after Palpatine became Emperor, a story circulated that

Vader had tracked down a nest of fifty Jedi traitors and killed every one of them by himself. Eyewitnesses described him as a wraithlike being who seemed to possess Jedi powers and wielded a lightsaber, but he was definitely not a Jedi. After all, the Jedi may have attempted to overthrow the Republic, but they had never been known to strangle their opponents.

Some suspected Darth Vader was a droid engineered to carry out the Emperor's will. Others suggested that he might have once been a professional gladiator or bounty hunter. There was even speculation that he might be a well-known public figure who had assumed the name "Darth Vader" and wore his face-concealing helmet to hide his true identity.

Vader himself did nothing to reveal his personal history. As far as he was concerned, the only thing people had to know about him was that he answered only to the Emperor.

As the Emperor's lieutenant, Vader carried out his Master's directives with lethal precision. Besides hunting Jedi, he supervised the expansion of the Imperial Navy and enforced every new law — many of which promoted the hatred of nonhumans — to bring greater power to the Empire. Those who opposed or disappointed Vader wound up dead or enslaved, and even Palpatine's most ardent supporters regarded the masked, shadowy cyborg with dread. In a short time, his very name became synonymous with terror.

The Emperor reorganized the Galactic Senate as the Imperial Senate, so he could continue to monitor and manipulate the representatives of the worlds he now controlled. Vader accompanied the Emperor to the more important Senate functions, which were often attended by Senator Bail Organa of Alderaan, among others. During the Clone Wars, Anakin Skywalker had, for a time, shared Senator Amidala's regard for Organa as a rare, honorable politician, but to Darth Vader, the man was as insignificant as a common insect. Like most people, Organa directed his gaze elsewhere when Vader was present.

After allocating the more mundane responsibilities of government to paranoid administrators, the Emperor made fewer public appearances, which allowed him to devote more of his time to studying the dark side of the Force in his palace on Coruscant. In time, Vader's looming form became the ultimate icon of Imperial authority.

But the Emperor never let Vader forget who was in charge. Over time, they had many variations of the same conversation, which usually began with the Emperor's taunting question: "Are you afraid of death, Lord Vader?"

"No, Master."

"Then why do you go on living?"

"To learn to become more powerful, Master."

"Do you seek such power so you might try to strike me down?"

"You are my path to power, Master. I need you."

"Yes, my apprentice. Remember your place, and that you have much to learn."

Vader eventually created his own private retreat, Bast Castle, on the storm-scoured planet Vjun, where Count Dooku had once taken refuge during the Clone Wars. On Vjun, Vader conducted his own studies of the dark side. He had no doubt that the Emperor knew what he wanted more than anything: the power to kill his Master. But because Palpatine was so incredibly powerful, and despite several attempts, Vader learned that he had no reason to believe he could ever defeat the elder Sith Lord.

As the years passed, the Empire expanded by conquering more worlds. While cloned soldiers were still utilized for the Imperial Navy, humans also began serving as enlisted officers or were conscripted into duty as technicians, pilots, and stormtroopers.

Although Anakin Skywalker had never had any personal exchanges with the bounty hunter Jango Fett, Darth Vader did become familiar with Fett's cloned "son," Boba Fett, who had inherited his father's armor, weapons, and starship. As Boba Fett gained a well-deserved reputation as the best bounty hunter in the galaxy, it was inevitable that Vader would occasionally retain him for clandestine assignments.

Vader also supervised secret operations on numerous worlds. To enlist deadly Noghri warriors to his cause, he came to the aid of their planet *after* he had covertly poisoned it with life-inhibiting toxins. When an Imperial research station accidentally released a lethal bioagent on the planet Falleen, Vader commanded his soldiers to fire turbolasers at the contaminated world, killing over two hundred thousand Falleen natives.

Of all the operations that Darth Vader oversaw, the most important was the construction of the Death Star, a moon-sized battle station that, when finished, would be equipped with a superlaser capable of destroying entire planets. Conceived by one of the Empire's highest-ranking officers, Grand Moff Wilhuff Tarkin, and originally designed on Geonosis, the Death Star promised to be the Empire's ultimate weapon. As part of Tarkin's doctrine of Rule by Fear, the battle station would strike such terror throughout the galaxy that no world would dare defy or disobey an Imperial command.

As Palpatine had foreseen, the Empire *did* have its enemies. One particular underground movement — the Alliance to Restore the Republic, more commonly known as the Rebel Alliance — proved to be the most irritating. Although Imperial officials were certain that the Rebels had established a secret base, the base's location remained unknown.

Nineteen years after the end of the Clone Wars and the birth of the Empire, the Rebel Alliance attacked an Imperial convoy in the Toprawa system in the Outer Rim. Darth Vader immediately realized that it had been a diversionary tactic, and that the Rebels' real goal was to infiltrate an Imperial research station on Toprawa.

The Rebels had stolen the plans for the Death Star.

CHAPTER FOURTEEN

Darth Vader had encountered Bail Organa's daughter, Princess Leia, at several occasions in recent years. The first time had been on Coruscant, before she had become a Senator, when she and her father had been standing in a receiving line to meet the Emperor at the Imperial Palace. Like most people, she had trembled in the Emperor's presence, and had given Vader no reason to assume she might pose any threat. Most recently, he had seen her and one of her officers, Captain Antilles, on the planet Ralltiir, where the Princess had claimed to be working as a goodwill ambassador, hoping to deliver medical supplies to Ralltiir's High Council. Because her recent movements had placed her in areas where there had been Rebel activity, Vader had made sure that her old Corellian Corvette — Imperials had given the make its nickname "Blockade Runner" because of its evasive qualities — did not leave Ralltiir without a tiny stowaway homing device.

After learning that the Rebels had attacked an Imperial convoy in the Toprawa system, Vader traveled swiftly there. He was standing beside his aide, the black-uniformed Commander Praji, on the bridge of the Imperial Star Destroyer *Devastator* in orbit of Toprawa, when a small blip that represented an incoming ship appeared on a sensor screen. Although the ship was not broadcasting an identification number, a homing signal indicated it was Princess Leia's Blockade Runner.

Vader was not surprised.

Seconds later, an Imperial communications officer looked up from his monitor and said, "Commander, scrambled transmissions are being sent from the planet."

Vader turned his helmet to face Praji and said, "The starship that just entered the system. Detain it."

Praji moved to a communications console to open a line to the Blockade Runner and spoke into a comlink, "Unidentified ship. Heave to at once and prepare for security search and interrogation!"

"This is the *Tantive IV*," a man's voice answered from the comlink, and Vader immediately recognized the speaker as Captain Antilles. "We have an extravehicular malfunction. A maintenance unit is working on it now." After a moment's pause, Antilles continued, "We are a consular ship on a diplomatic mission and will clear this system as soon as we have effected repairs."

Commander Praji looked to Vader, who gave a single approving nod. Returning to the comlink, Praji replied, "We acknowledge your transmissions, *Tantive IV*. The *Devastator* will hold fire. Maintain your present course and prepare to receive Imperial investigators."

A few seconds later, Antilles responded, "Imperial cruiser *Devastator*, we are on a diplomatic mission and are not to be detained or diverted."

Praji quickly examined a sensor screen. "*Tantive IV* has raised its energy shields and is accelerating out of orbit."

"After them," Vader ordered, confident that the Blockade Runner would not escape.

As the *Devastator*'s engines roared to life, Praji spoke again into the comlink. "*Tantive IV*, this is the *Devastator*. Our sensors indicate you have intercepted illegal transmissions in this solar system. Heave to or we'll open fire!"

When Vader saw that the Blockade Runner was maintaining its course, he said calmly, "Shoot for minimum damage."

The *Devastator*'s cannons launched long streaks of energized bolts that hammered at the small fleeing ship's shields. A moment later, the *Tantive IV*'s engines flared and the ship vanished into hyperspace.

Every spacer knew that it was impossible to track another ship through hyperspace, the dimension that allowed for travel at faster than lightspeed.

On the *Devastator*, Commander Praji consulted a sensor screen to locate the homing device. "Lord Vader, they're heading for the Tatooine system."

Tatooine! Vader appeared impassive, but behind his mask, he clenched his teeth and seethed. The very thought of Tatooine released a small flood of distasteful memories. Regaining his composure, Vader said, "Plot a course."

"Yes, my Lord."

By the time the *Tantive IV* reached the Tatooine system, the *Devastator* was right behind it. The Blockade Runner returned laserfire as it reached Tatooine's orbit, but was overwhelmingly outgunned by the Imperial Star Destroyer. After the Star Destroyer blasted away the Blockade Runner's primary sensor array and starboard shield projector, the smaller ship was effectively crippled.

An Imperial tractor beam drew the *Tantive IV* into the *Devastator*'s main hangar, and stormtroopers armed with blaster rifles were dispatched into the captured vessel. Several stormtroopers were shot down by the *Tantive IV*'s crew upon entry, but the steady stream of unrelenting white-armored Imperial soldiers managed to secure the ship within minutes.

When the blaster fight was over, Darth Vader boarded the *Tantive IV*. The white-walled corridors were scorched, the air was heavy with the scent of blaster fumes, and the floor was littered with the bodies of fallen stormtroopers as well as Rebel troops. Vader moved forward through the corridor like a malevolent shadow.

Captain Antilles had survived the Imperial assault and was escorted by stormtroopers to the ship's operations forum, where Vader was waiting for him. Vader wrapped his black-gloved fingers around Antilles's neck as an Imperial officer rushed up and announced, "The Death Star plans are not in the main computer."

Vader turned his visor to gaze at Captain Antilles. "Where are those transmissions you intercepted?" Without effort, the Sith Lord slowly raised his arm and lifted Antilles off the floor. "What have you done with those plans?"

Gasping, Antilles answered, "We intercepted no transmissions. Aaah . . . this is a consular ship. We're on a diplomatic mission."

Vader tightened his grip and said, "If this is a consular ship . . . where is the Ambassador?"

When Antilles did not answer, Vader decided the interrogation was over. The Dark Lord gave a sharp squeeze, instantly breaking Antilles's neck. Vader threw the corpse against the wall, and then turned to a stormtrooper.

"Commander," Vader said, "tear this ship apart until you've found those plans, and bring me the passengers. I want them alive!"

Minutes after the stormtroopers had begun their search for the passengers, Vader was informed that Princess Leia had been apprehended.

"Darth Vader," Leia addressed her captor. Her wrists were secured in binders and she ignored the numerous stormtroopers who also stood in the narrow corridor of the *Tantive IV*. Bravely staring straight into the dark lenses of the Sith Lord's helmet, she continued, "Only you could be so bold. The Imperial Senate will not sit still for this. When they hear you've attacked a diplomatic —"

"Don't act so surprised, Your Highness," Vader interrupted. "You weren't on any mercy mission this time. Several transmissions were beamed to this ship by Rebel spies. I want to know what happened to the plans they sent you."

"I don't know what you're talking about," Leia replied tersely. "I'm a member of the Imperial Senate on a diplomatic mission to Alderaan. . . ."

"You are a part of the Rebel Alliance . . . and a traitor," Vader snarled. "Take her away!"

As the stormtroopers led Leia from her ship to the Star Destroyer, a black-uniformed, hawk-nosed Imperial officer named Daine Jir trailed alongside Vader as the Sith Lord wound through the corridors, searching for some sign that might lead him to the stolen plans.

"Holding her is dangerous," said the outspoken Jir. "If word of this gets out, it could generate sympathy for the Rebellion in the Senate."

"I have traced the Rebel spies to here," Vader said without concern. "Now she is my only link to finding their secret base."

Jir must have been aware of the Princess's reputation, for he added, "She'll die before she'll tell you anything."

"Leave that to me," Vader said. "Send a distress signal and then inform the Senate that all aboard were killed!"

As Vader arrived at a corridor intersection, Commander Praji stopped him and said, "Lord Vader, the battle station plans are not aboard this ship! And no transmissions were made. An escape pod was jettisoned during the fighting, but no life-forms were aboard."

Feeling his anger rise, Vader said, "She must have hidden the plans in the escape pod. Send a detachment down to retrieve them. See to it personally, Commander. There'll be no one to stop us this time."

"Yes, sir," said Praji.

"And send detachments to secure the planet's spaceports," Vader added. "No ship is to leave Tatooine without Imperial authorization."

Vader stepped to a viewport and gazed down at the sand planet. It looked just as barren as he remembered it.

To think that I lived there once . . . that it was my home before the Jedi came and took me away. My mother breathed her last on this world, and for years I felt such . . . agonizing loss.

Now I feel nothing. This world means as much to me as a speck of dust, and all its inhabitants might as well be dust too.

As he returned to the *Devastator*, Vader considered the fact that Tatooine *could* be reduced to dust by the Death Star. He wondered if watching the sand planet's obliteration might bring him any pleasure. It was a possibility he wouldn't rule out.

CHAPTER FIFTEEN

An orb that was 160 kilometers in diameter, the Death Star was the size of a Class IV moon and was the largest starship ever built. Its quadanium steel outer hull had two prominent features: a concave superlaser focus lens set into the upper hemisphere, and an equatorial trench that contained ion engines, hyperdrives, and hangar bays. Besides its superlaser, which was not yet fully operational, the Death Star's weaponry included more than 10,000 turbolaser batteries, 2,500 laser cannons, and 2,500 ion cannons. Its hangars contained 7,000 Twin Ion Engine starfighters and more than 20,000 military and transport vessels. The battle station's crew, troops, and pilots numbered over one million.

The Death Star did not in any way impress Darth Vader.

After returning from the Tatooine system with Princess Leia as his prisoner, Vader and the hollow-cheeked Grand Moff Tarkin entered a Death Star conference room where a meeting was already in progress. Admiral Motti, the senior Imperial commander in charge of operations on the Death Star, General Tagge of the Imperial Army, and five other high-ranking Imperial officials sat around a table and listened as Tarkin announced that the Emperor had dissolved the Imperial Senate, and assured them that fear of the Death Star would keep the local star systems in line.

While General Tagge maintained concern that the Rebel Alliance might use the stolen Death Star plans to their advantage, Admiral Motti snidely asserted that any attack against the Death Star would be a useless gesture. "This station is now the ultimate power in the universe," Motti said. "I suggest we use it."

"Don't be too proud of this technological terror you've constructed," Vader cautioned. "The ability to destroy a planet is insignificant next to the power of the Force."

Sneering at the Sith Lord, Motti said, "Don't try to frighten us with your sorcerer's ways, Lord Vader. Your sad devotion to that ancient religion has not helped you conjure up the stolen data tapes or given you clairvoyance enough to find the Rebels' hidden fort —"

Motti stopped speaking and reached to his throat as Vader made a pinching movement with his own gloved hand from across the meeting room. "I find your lack of faith disturbing," Vader said.

"Enough of this!" Tarkin snapped. "Vader, release him!"

Although Vader answered only to the Emperor, it was the Emperor's command that he serve Tarkin on the Death Star. "As you wish," Vader said as he lowered his hand, releasing his telekinetic grip on Motti's throat.

Gasping for air, Motti slumped forward onto the table. Tarkin said, "This bickering is pointless. Lord Vader will provide us with the location of the Rebel fortress by the time this station is operational. We will then crush the Rebellion with one swift stroke!"

After the meeting, Vader was informed that he had an incoming message from the Tatooine system. He had already been notified that Commander Praji's stormtrooper squad had learned that the *Tantive IV*'s missing escape pod had carried two droids to Tatooine's surface, and that the droids had been picked up by a Jawa sandcrawler. Vader walked over to a communications console, where a holoprojector flickered to life and projected an image of two fully armed Imperial sandtroopers standing beside a middle-aged man and woman who wore robes and were kneeling on the ground. Near the four figures, there was a partial view of a structure, which Vader recognized as an entry dome for a desert dwelling.

Addressing the sandtrooper squad leader, Vader said, "Report via closed circuit."

"Lord Vader," said one of the sandtroopers, adjusting a control on his helmet so that only Vader could hear his voice. "The Jawas sold a protocol droid and an astromech to these moisture farmers, but both droids are gone."

Moisture farmers? Intrigued, Vader examined the holograms of the kneeling couple and said, "The farmers' names?"

"Owen and Beru Lars, sir," the sandtrooper responded. "They say they don't know where the droids are, but it looks like a landspeeder is missing from their garage."

Owen and Beru, Vader recalled. The resolution of their holograms was clear enough that he could make out their worn, weathered features. Neither of them appeared to be comfortable having blaster rifles aimed at their backs. Remembering how they'd looked on the day Anakin Skywalker had met them, Vader thought, *The years have not been kind. It's time for them to pay for their repeated weaknesses.*

"Your orders, sir?" said the sandtrooper.

"Tell Mr. and Mrs. Lars that they seem to have trouble keeping protocol droids on their property."

Not certain if he had heard correctly, the sandtrooper said, "Sir?"

"Then you may extend to them every courtesy that you showed the Jawas before you continue your search. Establish checkpoints to detain any droids entering Mos Espa or Mos Eisley spaceports. And one more thing."

"Yes, Sir?"

"Do not stop transmitting until I break the connection."

"Understood," said the sandtrooper.

Vader watched the sandtroopers carry out his orders on their helpless victims. He found the sight of rising flames — even holograms of flames burning millions of light years away — to be most satisfying.

When the Lars family homestead had been transformed into an inferno, Vader deactivated the holo-projector. He proceeded to the nearest lift tube, and was quickly transported to sublevel five of detention area AA-23, which was reserved for political prisoners.

Time to talk with the Princess.

The door to detention cell 2187 slid up into the ceiling and Darth Vader ducked through the doorway, followed by two black-uniformed Imperial soldiers. Inside the cell, Princess Leia sat on a bare metal bed that projected from the wall. Looming over the prisoner, Vader said, "And now, Your Highness, we will discuss the location of your hidden Rebel Base."

There was an electric hum from behind Vader, then a spherical black interrogator droid hovered slowly into the cell. The droid's midsection was ringed by a repulsorlift system, and its exterior was festooned with devices that included an electroshock assembly, sonic torture device, chemical syringe, and lie determinator.

Leia's eyes went wide at the sight of the droid, and Vader could practically taste her terror. She said, "Keep it away from me!"

Vader seized his prisoner, pinning her arms to her sides while the interrogator droid moved in closer. There was a brief hiss from the droid's injector arm, then Leia cried out and fell backward, slumping against the cell wall with a thud. "You can't . . ." she said. "You c —"

"Your Highness," Vader said in his most soothing tone. "Listen to my voice."

Leia's eyes rolled in their sockets, unable to focus on anything. She stammered, "V-voice . . ."

"That's right. Listen . . . I am your friend."

"Wha — friend?" Leia said, then winced. "No . . ."

"Yes!" Vader insisted, watching her plunge deeper into a hypnotic state. "You trust me, you can confide in me. All your secrets are safe with me."

"Mmmm?" Leia licked her lips. "Safe?"

"That's right, safe. You are safe here. You're among friends. You can trust me. I am a member of the Rebel Alliance, like you."

A look of relief swept over Leia's face as she muttered, "Rebel?"

"What did you do with the Death Star plans? Where are they? The Rebels need to know! Help us, Leia!"

"No," she moaned, closing her eyes. "Can't!"

"It's your duty," Vader urged. "Your duty to our Alliance. Your obligation to Alderaan and to your father. It's your duty to tell us where those tapes are!"

"Father?" Leia said, her eyes still shut.

"Yes," Vader said. "Your father commands you to tell us!"

"Father . . . wouldn't."

Growing impatient, Vader used his own psychic powers to make Leia believe she was in excruciating pain, but after several minutes, he ended the interrogation. He sensed that her inborn willpower was not only formidable but must have been augmented with certain physical and mental disciplines. She would not be broken easily.

Leaving the detention cell, he went to report to Grand Moff Tarkin in the Death Star control room. Vader said, "Her resistance to the mind probe is considerable. It will be some time before we can extract any information from her."

Just then, Admiral Motti approached Tarkin and informed him that the Death Star was finally fully operational. Tarkin looked to Vader and said, "Perhaps she would respond to an alternative form of persuasion."

"What do you mean?" asked Vader.

"I think it's time we demonstrated the full power of this station," Tarkin said. Turning to Motti, he commanded, "Set your course for Alderaan."

"With pleasure," Motti replied with an evil smile.

Realizing what Tarkin intended, Vader surveyed the man with new respect. The Dark Lord had done many horrendous and unpardonable things, but it seemed that Tarkin — at least in this situation — was even more diabolically inventive. However, Vader had one concern with Tarkin's scheme. "Alderaan is one of the foremost of the inner systems," Vader said. "The Emperor should be consulted."

"Do not think to challenge *me*!" Tarkin snapped. "You are not confronting Tagge or Motti now! The Emperor has placed me in charge of this affair with a free hand, and the decision is mine! And you will have your information that much sooner."

Vader had long suspected that Grand Moff Tarkin was insane, but it was not until Tarkin had addressed him just then, without a trace of fear, that Vader was left without a doubt. Vader said, "If your plan serves our purpose, it will justify itself."

"The stability of the Empire is at stake," Tarkin said. "A planet is a small price to pay."

Released from her cell and brought to Grand Moff Tarkin in the Death Star control room, Princess Leia stood against Darth Vader's chest with her eyes fixed on a wide viewscreen that displayed the planet Alderaan. After Tarkin threatened to destroy her homeworld unless she revealed the location of the Rebel base, she told them that the Rebels were on Dantooine. However, Tarkin was determined to prove that the Empire was prepared to use the Death Star without the slightest provocation.

There were billions of people on Alderaan, including Bail Organa, and they were all about to die. As the battle station's superlaser powered up, Vader felt the Princess quivering with fear.

You brought this upon yourself, he thought.

The green-beamed superlaser fired at Alderaan, blowing the entire world to oblivion.

CHAPTER SIXTEEN

After the Princess was returned to her cell, Vader met with Tarkin in the Death Star conference room. Tarkin said, "What of the search for the plans?"

"I am convinced that the Princess sent them down to the planet Tatooine with a pair of droids. A short time ago, a starship made a highly illegal blastoff from the Mos Eisley spaceport on Tatooine after her crew exchanged fire with a squad of stormtroopers. The ship then entered hyperspace, evading pursuit. The droids in question were thought to be aboard her."

Tarkin grimaced. "And our stormtroopers were outfought, our Starfleet evaded? How is this possible? Whose ship was it?"

"That is difficult to say," Vader said. "She had false identification markings and a forged registration. Moreover, she was an extremely fast and elusive vessel, probably one of the smugglers who congregate in that region."

An Imperial officer entered the conference room and reported that scout ships had traveled to Dantooine but discovered only the remains of a Rebel base that had been deserted for some time. After the officer left, Tarkin exploded with rage.

"She lied!" Tarkin snarled. "She lied to us!"

As much as Vader respected Tarkin's indifference to mass murder, the Grand Moff's rattled outburst indicated that Princess Leia had clearly won this particular battle of wills. Unable to resist driving a splinter into Tarkin's demented psyche, Vader said, "I *told* you she would never consciously betray the Rebellion."

Tarkin scowled at Vader. "Terminate her . . . immediately!"

Vader moved across the conference room to a communications console. With his helmet facing the comlink, he said, "Detention Area Security. Schedule the prisoner in cell 2187 for execution in one standard hour."

"Yes, Lord Vader," answered a voice from the comlink.

Glaring at Vader's back, Tarkin said, "I said *immediately*, Lord Vader."

Vader was about to respond when a comlink buzzed on the table in front of Tarkin. He pushed a button and said, "Yes?"

From the comlink, an Imperial officer announced, "We've captured a freighter entering the remains of the

Alderaan system. Its markings match those of a ship that blasted out of Mos Eisley."

Processing the information, Vader hypothesized, "They must be trying to return the stolen plans to the Princess. She may yet be of some use to us."

Vader proceeded to Death Star Docking Bay 327, where a tractor beam had deposited the captured ship. Entering the large hangar, Vader recognized the battered vessel as an old Corellian YT-1300 stock light freighter. He also noted its customized features, including illegal military-grade blaster cannons and an absurdly large top-of-the-line sensor dish on the port side.

Definitely a smuggler's ship, Vader thought as he walked past the squad of stormtroopers who were guarding the ship.

A gray-uniformed Imperial captain and a pair of stormtroopers stepped down the ship's landing ramp. Stopping before Vader, the captain said, "There's no one on board, sir. According to the log, the crew abandoned ship right after takeoff. It must be a decoy, sir. Several of the escape pods have been jettisoned."

"Did you find any droids?"

"No, sir," the captain replied. "If there were any on board, they must also have been jettisoned."

"Send a scanning crew aboard," Vader ordered. "I want every part of the ship checked."

"Yes, sir."

Vader looked up at the ship's hull. "I sense something . . . a presence I've not felt since . . ."

Since Mustafar.

Then it hit him.

Obi-Wan Kenobi . . .

He's alive!

Nearly an hour after the freighter had been captured, Grand Moff Tarkin was at his usual place in the conference room when Darth Vader announced: "He is here."

"Obi-Wan Kenobi!" Tarkin said with disbelief. "What makes you think so?"

"A tremor in the Force," Vader answered. "The last time I felt it was in the presence of my old Master."

"Surely he must be dead by now."

"Don't underestimate the power of the Force."

"The Jedi are extinct," Tarkin insisted. "Their fire has gone out of the universe. You, my friend, are all that's left of their religion." A signal chimed from the comlink at the console in front of Tarkin's seat. Tarkin pressed a console button and said, "Yes?"

From the comlink, a voice said, "We have an emergency alert in detention block AA-23."

"The Princess!" Tarkin exclaimed. "Put all sections on alert!"

"Obi-Wan *is* here," Vader said. "The Force is with him."

"If you're right, he must not be allowed to escape."

"Escape is not in his plan," Vader said knowingly. "I must face him — alone." He turned for the door. As large as the Death Star was, he knew he would find the elusive Jedi Master.

But first, he would make certain that a homing device was placed on the captured freighter. Although he was confident that Obi-Wan wouldn't leave the Death Star, he was actually counting on the possibility that the Princess would.

Obi-Wan Kenobi, wearing a dirty-brown desert robe with a large cloak, had bypassed numerous stormtroopers and sophisticated security sensors by the time Vader sighted him, entering the dimly illuminated, gray-walled access tunnel that led back to Docking Bay 327. Vader stood in plain sight, holding his red-bladed lightsaber at the ready, blocking Obi-Wan's path to the captured freighter.

He looks so old, Vader thought, but knew better than to assume that the white-bearded Obi-Wan had weakened with age. As Vader moved slowly toward the hooded interloper, Obi-Wan activated his own blue-bladed lightsaber.

"I've been waiting for you, Obi-Wan," Vader said, edging closer to the elderly Jedi. "We meet again, at last. The circle is now complete."

Obi-Wan assumed an offensive stance.

"When I left you," Vader continued, "I was but the learner; now I am the master."

"Only a master of evil, Darth," Obi-Wan said.

Although Vader had not expected Obi-Wan to address him by the obsolete name of Anakin Skywalker, it was most unusual for anyone to call him by his Sith Lord title alone. Vader thought, *He's trying to confuse me!*

Obi-Wan moved fast, lunging at Vader with his weapon, but the Dark Lord blocked the attack with ease. There was a loud electric crackle as their lightsabers made contact. Undeterred, Obi-Wan made a swift series of strikes, but each was parried by Vader.

"Your powers are weak, old man," Vader said.

"You can't win, Darth," Obi-Wan said, making Vader wonder if perhaps Obi-Wan was taunting him by refusing to address him properly. With incredible self-assurance, Obi-Wan added, "If you strike me down, I shall become more powerful than you can possibly imagine."

"You should *not* have come back," Vader said.

Their lightsabers clashed again and again, and their duel carried on until they were just outside Docking Bay 327. As they moved toward the door that led directly into the hangar that contained the captured freighter, Vader heard the approaching footsteps of stormtroopers running toward his position. Vader's blade was crossed with his opponent's when Obi-Wan threw a glance into the hangar. Vader kept his eyes riveted on the Jedi. *You won't get away from me this time!*

Unexpectedly, Obi-Wan raised his lightsaber before him and closed his eyes. His expression was serene.

Vader could hardly believe it. *He's surrendering!* Without mercy, Vader swung hard with his lightsaber, slicing through Obi-Wan's form. He fully expected to hear the satisfying sound of Obi-Wan's ruined body collapsing upon the polished floor, and so was astonished to see only the Jedi's robe and lightsaber at his feet. Obi-Wan's body had completely vanished.

"No!" a voice shouted from the hangar. Suddenly, the hangar was filled with the rapid reports of many blasters firing at the same time.

Vader heard the shout and the blasters but he paid them no attention. Astonished, he stared at Obi-Wan's weapon and empty robe, then prodded the clothes with his boot. *Where is he? How could he vanish? What sort of trickery is this?*

From the hangar, over the din of the blaster fight, Vader heard Princess Leia call out, "Come on! Come on! Luke, it's too late!"

Vader had no interest in stopping Princess Leia, nor did he wonder who "Luke" might be. But he couldn't let them get away too easily. Turning away from Obi-Wan's fallen robe and lightsaber, he headed for the hangar. But before he could reach the doorway, a man's voice in the hangar shouted, "Blast the door, kid!"

There was a small explosion outside the doorway, and the two blast doors slid out from the walls to seal off the hangar. Moments later, Vader heard the freighter's engines roar to life, carrying the ship out of the hangar and away from the Death Star.

It had been Vader's idea to plant the homing device on the freighter, and to allow the Princess to escape so she would unwittingly lead the Imperials to the secret Rebel base. Vader had been confident that his plan would work. And yet as he picked up Kenobi's lightsaber, he realized that he was now less certain of what the future held.

It was determined that the freighter had traveled to Yavin 4, the same moon where Anakin Skywalker had dueled Asajj Ventress during the Clone Wars. *First Tatooine, now Yavin 4*, Vader thought. Despite his devotion to the power of the dark side of the Force, he had the nagging sense that his past was coming back to haunt him.

Once the Death Star arrived in the Yavin system and was within thirty minutes' range of destroying the moon with the Rebel base, Vader's confidence returned.

"Today will be a day long remembered," he told Tarkin in the Death Star control room. "It has seen the end of Kenobi. It will soon see the end of the Rebellion."

By the time the Imperial tactical officers had deter-mined that the stolen technical readouts revealed a vulnerable area of their battle station, dozens of Rebel starfighters had already begun their assault on the Death Star. Tarkin and most of his men had regarded the enemy ships as nothing more than a temporary nui-sance, but Darth Vader had felt his confidence shift again as the battle progressed. Vader had never consid-ered the Death Star as anything more than a deadly, oversized toy, but because the expensive superweapon was necessary for the Emperor's schemes, he had been duty-bound to protect it.

And he had failed.

Now, as the Super Star Destroyer Executor *arrived in the Endor system, he thought back on what had hap-pened at Yavin four years ago.*

With Obi-Wan Kenobi's lightsaber clipped to his belt like a trophy, he had flown his bent-winged prototype

TIE fighter to defend the Death Star. None of the Rebel pilots had been a match for him until he had caught up with a single X-wing fighter in the Death Star's equatorial trench. Despite the fury of the space battle, Vader had easily sensed that the Force was strong with this one X-wing pilot. Vader had been about to fire at his evasive target when an unexpected blast from above damaged his own ship and sent him spinning out into space. He had but a millisecond to see that he had been attacked by the same freighter that had led the Death Star to Yavin.

And then the Death Star had exploded. The resulting shock wave had sent his TIE fighter tumbling further and faster from Yavin. It had not taken him long to regain control of his ship, but because the freighter's attack had crippled his hyperdrive and communications systems, it was some time before he reached an Imperial outpost. Vader had used that time to think about the droids that Princess Leia had sent to Tatooine, and the freighter that had transported Obi-Wan Kenobi to the Death Star. Vader had wondered, How long was Obi-Wan on Tatooine. And why?

Had he been in contact with Owen and Beru Lars?

Did Princess Leia know that he was alive, and that the droids would find him there?

And the Rebel pilot who was so strong with the Force . . . where had he come from?

The Emperor had not been pleased to learn of the

loss of the Death Star, but he had not faulted Vader. After all, Vader had nothing to do with the battle station's flawed design. While Palpatine's propaganda architects had launched a campaign to discredit the Rebel Alliance by denying that a moon-sized Imperial battle station ever existed, Vader had conducted his own investigation to identify the Rebel pilot who had destroyed the Death Star, and devised a plan to lure the Rebels to the Starship Yards of Fondor.

Vader had failed to capture the Rebel spy who took the bait at Fondor, but through the Force, Vader had sensed that the spy was the pilot who had eluded him at the Death Star, and that this individual had indeed been a disciple of Obi-Wan Kenobi.

Eventually, he had learned the pilot's name.

CHAPTER SEVENTEEN

Luke Skywalker.

According to municipal records obtained from the settlement of Anchorhead on Tatooine, that was the name on the registration for a T-16 skyhopper owned by a human male pilot who had lived at the Lars homestead and was approximately nineteen standard years old.

Luke Skywalker.

According to a Kubaz freelance spy in Mos Eisley, that was the name on a Spaceport Speeders sales record for the landspeeder that had been purchased from a young man who later left on the *Millennium Falcon*, the Corellian freighter that had also carried Obi-Wan Kenobi to the Death Star.

Luke Skywalker.

According to a captured Rebel whom Darth Vader interrogated on the planet Centares, that was the name of the X-wing pilot who had destroyed the Death Star.

Luke Skywalker.

Even while inspecting his nearly completed flagship, the Super Star Destroyer *Executor*, at the Starship Yards of Fondor, Vader could not get Luke Skywalker out of his mind. He silently chewed on the name, and considered the fact that the boy had been born three years *after* the death of Shmi Skywalker. To the best of his knowledge, Anakin Skywalker had been his mother's only living blood relative.

Could there have been other Skywalkers from Tatooine? Vader allowed the possibility. After all, it wasn't an entirely uncommon name in the galaxy.

But Anakin and Padmé Amidala had been expecting a baby nineteen years ago.

Nineteen standard years.

It's not possible, Vader thought. *I killed Padmé. The baby died with her.*

Not for the first time, he wondered if the Emperor had told him the whole truth about Padmé's death. *But I remember choking her . . . seeing her collapse on Mustafar. I was so angry with her. And yet . . .*

Luke Skywalker exists.

Vader refused to believe that the notorious Rebel's surname was merely a bizarre coincidence. If he had possessed any other name, Vader would not have hesitated to report what he had learned to the Emperor. But for purely selfish reasons, Vader kept the Rebel's name to himself. To him, Luke Skywalker was more than a mystery to be solved.

He is . . . an opportunity. As strong with the Force as he may be, he is an opportunity . . . an opportunity for even greater power.

But who is he? Who were his parents? Could he have been Obi-Wan's son? But then why was he named Skywalker and raised by the Lars family? Or was he merely trained by Obi-Wan?

Because Obi-Wan Kenobi, Shmi Skywalker, Owen and Beru Lars, and Padmé Amidala were dead, there was only one way Vader could discover the truth. He would have to ask Luke Skywalker himself. All he had to do was find him.

After enlisting an actor to impersonate Obi-Wan Kenobi, Vader tailored a new trap specifically for Luke on the desert world of Aridus. Unfortunately, Luke saw through the ruse and escaped. Vader was even more frustrated by the actions of his top officer, the ultimately incompetent Admiral Griff, who allowed the Rebel Alliance to evade the Imperial blockade at Yavin 4 and evacuate to a new secret base.

Vader was not idle as he searched and waited for any information that would lead him to Luke Skywalker and his allies. He brought Obi-Wan Kenobi's lightsaber back to Bast Castle, where he also studied an ancient Sith Holocron he had acquired. He oversaw various secret projects, including the development of mind-altering Pacifog on Kadril, the construction of robotic Imperial Dark Troopers, and preparation for a new superweapon in the Endor system. He assigned a Force-sensitive Imperial Intelligence agent named Shira Brie to infiltrate the Rebel Alliance, but her mission to discredit Luke Skywalker was a failure and left her horribly injured. Because Vader still considered Brie valuable, he ordered Imperial medics to replace her shattered limbs with cyborg prosthetics, and offered her to Palpatine to serve as an elite secret operative.

Luke Skywalker was not idle either. As word of his actions spread, many Imperials became familiar with the name of the young pilot who was a leading figure in the Rebel Alliance.

Two years after the destruction of the Death Star, an Imperial governor notified Vader that persons matching the descriptions of Luke Skywalker and Princess Leia Organa had been captured on Circarpous V, a swamp planet known locally as Mimban. Vader was aware of the Mimban legend about the Kaiburr Crystal, a luminous crimson-colored gem that magnified the Force a thousandfold, and hoped to collect this relic along with the captive Rebels.

By the time Vader arrived on Mimban, Skywalker and the Princess had escaped and fled into the jungle. After a close encounter in a cavern, he finally caught up with them at the vine-encrusted Temple of Pomojema, a pyramidal ziggurat constructed of great blocks of volcanic stone for an ancient Mimban deity, which contained the Kaiburr Crystal. Using the Force, Vader dropped a stone ceiling on Luke Skywalker, pinning him to the temple floor, while Leia Organa watched helplessly.

"You have a great deal to atone for to me," Vader told Skywalker, who, like the Princess, was attired in the dark work uniform worn by local miners. Activating his lightsaber, Vader began swinging its red blade back and forth, chopping playfully at bits of stone from the surrounding walls. "I probably won't have the patience to let you last as long as you deserve," he continued. "You may consider yourself lucky."

Turning his attention to the Princess, Vader said, "I expect no such difficulty in restraining myself where you are concerned, Leia Organa. In several ways, you are responsible for my setbacks much more than this simple boy."

Simple boy? Vader was surprised by the words that had come from his own mouth. Even though he knew there was more to Skywalker than met the eye, and had only intended on apprehending the Rebels, he was suddenly overcome by the desire to kill them. He realized he was losing his self-control.

The Princess picked up Luke's lightsaber and activated its blue blade. As she moved toward Vader, he abruptly let his arm fall, letting the beam of his own weapon hang limply at his side.

"Leia, don't!" Luke yelled. "It's a feint . . . he's daring you. Kill me, then yourself . . . it's hopeless now."

Gazing at the Princess with contempt, Vader said to her, "Go on, let him fight for you if you want. But I won't let you kill him." Thinking of how Luke had escaped his clutches before, he added, "I've been robbed too often."

The Princess fought bravely, but she was no match for Vader. She used the last of her strength to throw the lightsaber to Skywalker, just as he emerged from under the rubble. Facing the Sith Lord, Skywalker said, "Ben Kenobi is with me, Vader, and the Force is with me too."

The duel was furious, and carried Vader and Skywalker through the temple to a chamber where there was a dark circular opening in the floor, the mouth of a deep pit. As the battle wore on, Vader found himself breathing hard through his respirator. But then, thanks to his proximity to the Force-enhancing Kaiburr Crystal, he felt a sudden surge of the power of the dark side, allowing him to project lightning from his fingertips for the first time in his life. He hurled Force-energized lightning at Skywalker, but his young opponent deflected the blast.

"Not . . . possible!" Vader muttered, feeling his energy drain. "Such power . . . in a child. Not possible!"

As Skywalker threw himself at the towering black figure, Vader raised his lightsaber to defend himself. But he wasn't fast enough. Skywalker's blade cut through the Sith Lord's prosthetic right arm, and it fell to the floor, still clutching the red-bladed lightsaber.

Dazed, Vader bent and used his left hand to pry his weapon from the gloved fingers of his severed arm. He was shifting his weight to make another attack when he suddenly had a clear view of the lightsaber in Skywalker's grip. The weapon's design and handgrip looked . . . familiar.

Vader's head suddenly felt heavy, and as he tried to move forward, he stumbled over his severed limb. The robotic arm tumbled after him as he plummeted into the nearby pit.

He howled as he descended into the darkness, and it seemed like his fall would never end. Throughout the fall, he thought of Skywalker's lightsaber. Vader would have sworn it was the same weapon that Obi-Wan had taken from Anakin Skywalker on Mustafar. He didn't stop howling with rage until he crashed in a heap upon a pile of hard stones.

It was over an hour before Vader regained consciousness at the bottom of the pit below the Temple of Pomojema. He tasted blood inside his helmet and silently cursed himself.

He realized what had happened in the temple. The Kaiburr Crystal had increased his Force powers, but not to his advantage. It had amplified his hatred and anger, causing him to abandon his desire to capture Skywalker and find out more about his identity. Now he sensed that the Kaiburr Crystal was no longer in the temple, that it had left Mimban.

Along with Skywalker and the Princess.

Vader gathered up his arm and lightsaber, and made his way out of the cavern, where he summoned an Imperial shuttle to deliver him to the nearest medical center. Even as his right arm was replaced, he did not consider his battle on Mimban a loss, for now he knew that Skywalker was more than an opportunity for greater power: He was the solution to his greatest obstacle.

He's the one person who can help me overthrow the Emperor.

Vader had never discussed Luke Skywalker with the Emperor, but he did not rule out the possibility that his Master had learned the name of the Rebel pilot who had destroyed the Death Star. It was only a matter of time before the Emperor broached the subject.

Even though Vader had yet to discover any significant information about Skywalker's heritage, he did sense there was a strong connection between them, and not only because they had both been trained by Obi-Wan. But Vader didn't want simply more information. He wanted Skywalker, wanted him immediately, and wanted him alive.

It was therefore inevitable that the Dark Lord would meet with Boba Fett.

CHAPTER EIGHTEEN

Wearing the helmet and armor he'd inherited from his father, Boba Fett stood before Darth Vader in a spaceport reception room on Ord Mantell, a Mid Rim planet that had once been an ordinance depot for the Old Republic. The room had a wide window that overlooked the landing pad where Vader's *Lambda*-class shuttle was taking on supplies. Vader's own armor and inner workings had been fully repaired, leaving no evidence of his duel on Mimban.

"You seek certain Rebels, Lord Vader," Fett rasped through his helmet's vocabulator. "So does my employer, Jabba the Hutt. Possibly in satisfying him, I can satisfy you also."

"And collect two rewards instead of just one, bounty hunter?" said Vader, not missing a trick. "A particular Rebel interests me . . . Luke Skywalker."

Boba Fett gave a slight nod, tilting his helmet forward.

"A companion of the man I'm after . . . Han Solo. One might lure the other, Lord Vader."

By now, Vader was familiar with the name of the captain of the *Millennium Falcon*, the ship that had fired upon his TIE fighter at the Death Star battle. He was not interested in why Jabba the Hutt wanted Han Solo, but behind his black mask, he felt a grin twitch across his lips as he considered using Solo as bait for Skywalker. "You are enterprising, Fett," he said as he turned for a lift tube that led down to the landing pad. "Perhaps we will meet again when your enterprise bears fruit."

Leaving Fett on Ord Mantell, Vader returned to the *Executor*. Although he would be pleased if the bounty hunter's plan worked, he was unwilling to wait for information leading to the location of the new base for the Rebel Alliance. Finding Luke Skywalker had become more than a goal for Darth Vader. It had become his *purpose*.

Already, thousands of sensor-laden Imperial probe droids had been dispersed to remote worlds throughout the galaxy, and thousands more would be deployed within the coming weeks. Sooner or later, one of those probe droids would turn up something useful.

Three standard years had passed since the Death Star's destruction when Vader, standing on the bridge of the *Executor*, learned that a probe droid had transmitted images of a large power generator on an ice planet in the distant Hoth system. "That's it," Vader said. "The Rebels are there." He refused to listen to his pompous chief officer, Admiral Ozzel, who suggested the probe droid could have turned up anything other than the Rebel base. "That *is* the system," he insisted. "Set your course for the Hoth system."

Unfortunately, the Rebels had already begun an emergency evacuation of their base, while Darth Vader's armada raced to their destination via hyperspace. Even worse, Admiral Ozzel allowed the *Executor* to exit hyperspace too close to the Hoth system, triggering sensors that alerted the Rebels to the armada's arrival and allowed them to raise a planetary energy field to deflect any aerial bombardment. After relieving Ozzel of his life and promoting the more capable Captain Piett to the rank of Admiral, Vader gave the command to send Imperial troops down to the ice world's surface.

He's down there, Vader thought with absolute certainty. *Skywalker is down there.*

To their credit, the Rebels did not surrender on the spot. Their laser-firing snowspeeders swarmed the towering Imperial All Terrain Armored Transports that lumbered over the ice and snow, and their planetary ion cannon managed to disable the orbiting Imperial starships long enough for most of their fleet to escape into space. But in the end, they were unable to prevent the AT-ATs from destroying their power generators, and wave after wave of superior Imperial firepower ensured that the Rebels could never win the day.

It was hardly a victory for Vader, who landed on Hoth while the battle was still raging. The last of the Rebels were still fleeing from their vanquished base when he entered a cavernous, ice-walled hangar with a squad of snowtroopers, just in time to see the *Millennium Falcon* launching at high speed. Vader did not know whether Luke Skywalker had boarded Han Solo's freighter, but quickly sensed that Skywalker was still alive.

He had not forgotten Boba Fett's plan.

Turning to a snowtrooper, Vader said, "Alert Admiral Piett and all Star Destroyers that the *Millennium Falcon* is attempting to leave Hoth. Our primary objective is the capture of that freighter. The passengers are not to be harmed!"

Vader returned to the *Executor* and was seated in his meditation chamber when Admiral Piett entered his sanctum. As the robotic clamp lowered his helmet over his scarred head, Vader sensed Piett's discomfort at the sight of the Sith Lord's wounds. When the helmet was in place, Vader's seat rotated within the chamber until he faced Piett, who reported, "Our ships have sighted the *Millennium Falcon*, Lord. But . . . it has entered an asteroid field, and we cannot risk —"

"Asteroids do not concern me, Admiral," Vader interrupted. "I want that ship, not excuses."

Knowing better than to disagree with Vader, Piett said, "Yes, Lord."

The upper hemisphere of the meditation chamber descended over Vader. Hoping to gain some insight into events to come, he breathed slowly as he cleared his mind of all thoughts, opening himself to the dark side of the Force . . .

Skywalker.

He heard the name in his mind, as if the Force itself had whispered it to him. *But is it the Force*, Vader wondered, *or am I too preoccupied with finding —*

Suddenly, Vader sensed a disturbance in the Force. And not just a subtle fluctuation. Something major was about to happen, something incredibly significant . . .

Something that will change everything.

Asteroids were pummeling the Imperial fleet as Vader continued the search for the *Millennium Falcon*. Vader was on the bridge of the *Executor* when a very nervous Admiral Piett reported that the Emperor had commanded Vader to contact him.

Proceeding to his personal quarters, Vader stepped down to a circular black panel on the floor below his meditation chamber. The panel was a HoloNet scanner that allowed him to transmit communications across the galaxy. As he dropped to his left knee and bowed his helmeted head, the panel's outer ring became illuminated in a pale blue light. Vader slowly lifted his gaze to the empty air before him, and the emptiness was instantly filled by a large, flickering hologram of Emperor Palpatine's cloaked head.

"What is thy bidding, my Master?"

From light years away, on Coruscant, the Emperor replied, "There is a great disturbance in the Force."

"I have felt it," Vader said.

"We have a new enemy. The young Rebel who destroyed the Death Star. I have no doubt this boy is the offspring of Anakin Skywalker."

Offspring?! The surviving tissue in Vader's throat suddenly went dry. Through his shock, he managed to say, "How is that possible?"

Without offering any explanation to support his stated conviction, the Emperor answered, "Search your feelings, Lord Vader. You will know it to be true. He could destroy us."

Having fought Luke Skywalker on Mimban, Vader was even more aware of the young man's powers than was the Emperor. But he also knew something else: Luke was as ignorant of their familial connection as Vader had been. *If he had known the truth on Mimban,* Vader thought, *I would have sensed it.* Still grappling with the Emperor's declaration, he struggled to find words that might discourage his Master's interest in

Skywalker. "He is just a boy," Vader said. "Obi-Wan can no longer help him."

The Emperor believed otherwise. "The Force is strong with him," he said. "The son of Skywalker must not become a Jedi."

The Emperor had not said in so many words that he wanted Luke Skywalker dead, so Vader — needing Skywalker alive to accomplish his goals — took a different tact. "If he could be turned," Vader suggested, "he would become a powerful ally."

"Yes," the Emperor mused, as if he had not thought of this possibility. Vader could only imagine what the Emperor was thinking. The Sith had long maintained their rule of two: one Master, one apprentice. Even Vader knew that there wasn't room enough in the galaxy for three Sith Lords, and yet the Emperor's hooded eyes seemed to sparkle as he said more emphatically, "*Yes.* He would be a great asset. Can it be done?"

"He will join us or die, Master," Vader said. He bowed, and the Emperor's hologram faded out.

Now that the Emperor was interested in Luke Skywalker's fate, Vader knew he had to do everything in his power to find Luke before the Emperor found him. If his own soldiers and even the infamous Boba Fett could not locate the Rebel leaders, then he would have to take more proactive measures.

Vader sent out a signal, summoning bounty hunters from across the galaxy to meet him on the *Executor*. It was not long before six hunters, including Boba Fett, were lined up on the *Executor*'s bridge. Mere seconds after Vader addressed the assembled group and stressed that he wanted them to find the *Millennium Falcon* without killing anyone on board, the elusive Corellian freighter emerged from the asteroid field. The Star Destroyer *Avenger* gave chase, but moments later, the *Millennium Falcon* vanished from the *Avenger*'s tracking scopes. It seemed the Rebels had escaped once again from the Imperials.

But they didn't get away from Boba Fett. Several hours after the *Avenger* lost sight of the *Falcon*, Darth Vader received a transmission from Fett, who had employed stealthy measures to find the Rebel ship limping across space with a damaged hyperdrive, on course for the Bespin system.

Turning to Admiral Piett on the *Executor*'s bridge, the Dark Lord said, "Plot a course for Bespin."

CHAPTER NINETEEN

Boba Fett had already arrived at Cloud City, a luxury resort and gas refinery in orbit around the giant gas planet Bespin, and the lightspeed-disabled *Millennium Falcon* was still en route when Darth Vader's shuttle touched down on a Cloud City landing platform. Preceded by two squads of Imperial stormtroopers, Vader exited the shuttle to be greeted by Cloud City's Baron Administrator, Lando Calrissian, and his aide Lobot, a cyborg with a computer bracket wrapped around his bald head.

Calrissian was courteous and accommodating as he escorted the Imperials through his facility, and listened with attention when Vader outlined his plan to apprehend a group of Rebels. Upon hearing the name of the incoming Corellian freighter, Calrissian's expression remained completely neutral, which did not surprise Vader. Although a background check had confirmed that Calrissian was a former owner of the *Millennium Falcon*, he was also an accomplished gambler.

While the *Executor* remained stationed well out of scanner range of Bespin, the Imperials took up position within Cloud City and waited for Han Solo's ship to arrive. They didn't have to wait long.

"The *Millennium Falcon* has landed on Platform 327, Lord Vader," said Lieutenant Sheckil, a gray-uniformed Imperial officer. Sheckil was listening to an incoming progress report, and stood facing Vader and Fett in a Cloud City conference suite. "Princess Leia is with Captain Solo and his copilot," Sheckil continued. "There's a droid too. Baron Administrator Calrissian is leading them into Cloud City now." Sheckil smiled and added, "It was lucky the *Millennium Falcon*'s hyper-drive was damaged or we wouldn't have reached the Bespin system before the Rebels."

"Our journey to Bespin had nothing to do with *luck*, Lieutenant Sheckil," Vader said. "Remind your men to stay out of sight. The capture of the Rebels will be at my command."

"Yes, sir. I'll —" Sheckil stopped short as he listened to his comlink. "What? The imbeciles!" Trying not to sound nervous as he returned his attention to Vader, he said, "It's the droid, sir. It . . . it fell behind the group, and happened upon Gamma Squad's position. They . . .

blasted it. Fortunately, the Princess and the others didn't hear the shots."

"Then *you* are the only fortunate one," Vader seethed. "Do not fail me again. Bring the droid here at once. Its memory might contain valuable information."

After Sheckil left the room, Vader turned to gaze out a window at the Cloud City skyline. He said, "It seems your enterprise is bearing fruit, bounty hunter. By using Captain Solo as bait for Skywalker, you stand to collect two rewards instead of one."

Watching the Sith Lord's back, Boba Fett said, "Skywalker would get here faster if we spread word that his allies are in danger."

"That won't be necessary," Vader said, sensing a trembling in the Force from far across space. "He already *knows*."

Sheckil returned with a pair of stormtroopers who carried an open-topped container that held the captured droid's parts. The limbs had been torn from the torso, and a tangle of multicolored wires stuck out from the droid's neck socket.

"Lord Vader?" Sheckil said, "I-I'm afraid the damage is quite extensive." Holding the droid's head up for Vader's inspection, Sheckil continued, "As you can see, it's a protocol droid. Probably the Princess's property."

Vader took the head and examined it closely.

"The way these parts were shattered by the blast,"

Sheckil prattled on, "it's likely the droid was made a long time ago."

Despite the wear and tear to the droid's head, Vader recognized a few small details that indicated Anakin Skywalker's handiwork. He gazed into the decapitated head's blank photoreceptors.

C-3PO.

The last time Vader had seen the golden droid was on Mustafar. *I saw you through the window of Padmé's ship as it landed*, Vader recalled. Holding this relic of his former life, Vader felt waves of anger and loss sweep over his dark soul. His memory flashed to the day that Anakin had found the droid's skeleton in Watto's junkyard, and Anakin had wondered if the repaired droid might help him and his mother leave Tatooine.

Vader wondered whether C-3PO remembered anything of Anakin Skywalker. He doubted it. If the droid had had any knowledge of Anakin in his memory banks, then he would have shared that knowledge with Luke Skywalker. But Luke remained ignorant of his father's identity. Vader felt certain of that.

All things considered, Vader thought as he looked into the droid's eyes, *I should have left you in that scrap yard.* He had the sudden urge to crush the droid's head, but then realized that Sheckil and Boba Fett were watching him curiously.

Sheckil said, "Shall our technicians attempt to recover the unit's memory, Lord Vader?"

Relaxing his grip on the droid's head, Vader placed it with the other parts in the open container. "The droid is useless," he said. "Have it destroyed." He didn't give the droid another thought as he turned for the door and said, "Come, bounty hunter. I want to discuss our upcoming meeting with the Rebels."

After the tremor in the Force convinced Darth Vader that Luke Skywalker was on his way to Bespin, the Dark Lord sprung his trap. He arranged for Calrissian to escort Princess Leia, Han Solo, and Solo's Wookiee copilot to a banquet room where he and Boba Fett would be waiting. A moment after the banquet room's door slid open and revealed Darth Vader to the horrified Rebels, Solo reached for his blaster pistol and fired at the Sith Lord. With his gloved hand, Vader deflected the fired energy bolts, then used the Force to snatch Solo's pistol, tearing it from the pilot's grip so that it flew over the central banquet table to land in Vader's outstretched fingers.

"I had no choice," Calrissian told them. "They arrived right before you did. I'm sorry."

Solo glared at Calrissian and said, "I'm sorry too."

"Lord Vader!" Lieutenant Sheckil said with some excitement after the Sith Lord had exited the banquet room and ordered a stormtrooper squad to escort the prisoners to detention cells. "Our search of Princess Leia's quarters has turned up something . . . unexpected."

Walking fast with Sheckil in his wake, Vader made his way through the Cloud City corridors until they reached the spacious, brightly lit suite that Princess Leia had occupied before leaving for the banquet room. Two stormtroopers stood in the room beside two Ugnaughts: short, porcine humanoids who worked in the city's gas refineries. On top of a table rested a storage bin that held C-3PO's dismembered parts.

We meet again.

Staring at the parts, which looked no different from when he'd last seen them, Vader said, "I gave an *order*, Lieutenant."

"Yes, Lord Vader," Sheckil said. Gesturing to the squat workers, he continued, "But according to the Ugnaughts, the Wookiee broke into the junk room and went berserk when he found the parts. He brought them straight here to the Princess. If the Rebellion is interested in preserving this unit, there may be more to this droid than meets the eye."

Reaching into the storage bin, Vader picked up the droid's head. Despite his desire to leave all of Anakin Skywalker's memories buried, another one surfaced . . . something Shmi Skywalker had told her son after she had allowed him to keep the droid parts he had secretly hauled into their tiny hovel. She had said, *Unless you're prepared to care for something, you don't deserve to have it.*

Behind his helmet, Vader winced at the recollection.

Watching Vader, Sheckil said, "Shall I instruct the technicians to search its memory?" When Vader didn't answer, Sheckil added, "Or would you rather have the Ugnaughts smelt the thing?"

Vader seemed to continue contemplating the droid's head, holding it closer to his helmet so he could see his dark, distorted reflection on the weathered gold surface of C-3PO's lifeless face.

"Sir?" Sheckil said expectantly.

Darth Vader slowly placed the droid's head with the other parts. "The droid's parts carry the stench of Captain Solo's copilot," he said. "Deliver this box to the Wookiee's cell."

"I . . . forgive me, sir," Sheckil said, obviously confused. "I don't understand. You . . . want the prisoner to have the droid?"

"I am giving the Wookiee what he deserves," Vader said mysteriously.

"Oh," Sheckil said. "Yes . . . of course, Lord Vader."

"Captain Solo has an appointment in the interrogation chamber," Vader said as he strode for the suite's exit. "Make sure he gets there."

Vader did not ask a single question of Han Solo in the interrogation chamber that the Imperials had prepared on Cloud City, but he tortured the smuggler just the same. Afterward, he had a team of Ugnaughts prepare a carbon-freezing chamber for Solo, to determine whether Luke Skywalker could survive the freezing process. The test was also witnessed by Boba Fett, Lando Calrissian, Lobot, Princess Leia, and Solo's hulking copilot, who had already managed to partially reassemble C-3PO, carrying the droid's parts in a cargo net that was slung across his furry back. With some amusement, Vader noticed that C-3PO still didn't know when to stop talking.

Solo was lowered into the central pit of the freezing chamber, and there was a great blast of steam as he was instantly transformed into a solid block of carbonite. After the block was removed from the pit and Calrissian verified that Solo had survived in perfect hibernation, Vader turned to Boba Fett and said, "He's all yours, bounty hunter." Then he looked to the Ugnaughts and commanded, "Reset the chamber for Skywalker."

The timing could not have been better, for Skywalker had just landed his X-wing starfighter on Cloud City.

CHAPTER TWENTY

"The Force is strong with you, young Skywalker," Darth Vader said as his prey walked straight into his trap. "But you are not a Jedi yet."

Luke Skywalker had his blaster in hand as he entered the gloomy carbon-freezing chamber, but he holstered it before he climbed a flight of steps to stand before Vader. There, on the elevated platform that encircled the pit, Vader stood still, waiting for Skywalker to make his next move. When Luke reached for his lightsaber and ignited its blue blade, Vader noted that it was indeed the same weapon Obi-Wan had appropriated from Anakin Skywalker on Mustafar. But it wasn't time to share this information with Luke. Not yet.

Vader ignited his own lightsaber. Luke swung first, but Vader blocked the blow with ease. The duel was on.

Luke fought bravely, and even inventively, occasionally impressing Vader with unexpected moves. He even managed to leap out of the carbon-freezing chamber, preventing Vader from rendering him immobile. But Vader stalked him through Cloud City's reactor control room, used the Force to tear heavy machinery from the walls and hurl them at Luke, and ultimately drove him out onto a gantry that extended into the reactor shaft.

As the Bespin winds tore through the shaft, Luke swung his lightsaber to deliver a glancing blow on Vader's right shoulder plate. Vader snarled as Luke leaped farther out onto the gantry. Balanced on a narrow beam, Luke was clinging to a weather sensor with his left hand as Vader swung hard with his lightsaber.

Luke screamed as Vader's red blade swept through his right wrist, and watched with horror as his hand and lightsaber fell away into the deep reactor shaft.

"There is no escape," Vader said as his wounded opponent edged farther away to cling to a sensor array at the end of the gantry. "Don't make me destroy you," he added, increasing the volume of his voice so he could be heard over the high winds. "You do not yet realize your importance. You have only begun to discover your *power*. Join me, and I will complete your training. With our combined strength, we can end this destructive conflict and bring *order* to the galaxy."

"I'll never join you!" Luke screamed back.

"If only you knew the power of the dark side," Vader said, and decided that the time had come to reveal all. "Obi-Wan never told you what happened to your father."

"He told me enough!" Luke said through clenched teeth as he clung to the sensor array. "He told me you killed him."

"No," Vader said. "I *am* your father."

Darth Vader did not know how Luke would react. He could not imagine that the young man would be more shocked than Vader had been when the Emperor had informed him that Luke was Anakin Skywalker's son.

"No," Luke whimpered. "No. That's not true! That's impossible!"

Remembering how the Emperor had encouraged his acceptance, Vader said, "Search your feelings. You know it to be true."

"No!" Luke shouted. "NO!"

The wind howled, and Vader's black cape flapped wildly at his back. "Luke. You can destroy the Emperor. He has foreseen this. It is your *destiny*." He reached out to Luke, beckoning him to leave the gantry and come to his side. "Join me, and together we can rule the galaxy as father and son."

Still clinging to the sensor array, Luke glanced down the shaft.

"Come with me," Vader urged. "It is the *only* way."

Unexpectedly, Luke opened his arms, releasing the array and allowing himself to plummet into the deep shaft. Vader leaned out over the edge of the gantry to see his son's rapidly receding form tumble into an open exhaust pipe in the shaft's wall.

The Sith Lord was certain Luke was still alive. *If he had died, I would have sensed it.*

After Vader left the reactor shaft, Imperial officers informed him that the duplicitous Lando Calrissian had directed all residents and visitors to evacuate Cloud City, and that Calrissian, Princess Leia, and the Wookiee had already escaped in the *Millennium Falcon.* Vader knew they wouldn't get far, for Imperial technicians had already taken the precaution of disabling the *Millennium Falcon*'s hyperdrive.

Vader immediately dispatched two squads of stormtroopers to find Luke. Confident that Luke and the *Falcon*'s crew would soon be recovered and delivered to him, he made his way to his shuttle and flew back to the *Executor.* Upon his arrival, Vader remained confident when he was notified that the *Millennium Falcon* had raced back to Cloud City to rescue Luke.

Let his allies save him, Vader thought. *And then I shall capture them all.*

While the *Millennium Falcon* attempted to evade the Imperial blockade around Bespin, Vader used the Force to telepathically call out to his son from the *Executor*, "Luke."

Father, Luke called back.

"Son," Vader said, and felt a thrill as he realized Luke had accepted the truth.

As the Rebel freighter flew past Vader's Star Destroyer, Vader sensed Luke's proximity and used the

Force to call to him again. "Son. Come with me." When Luke did not respond, Vader added, "Luke. It is your destiny."

But then the *Millennium Falcon* vanished into hyperspace. And this time, the Corellian freighter was not carrying an Imperial tracking device.

Once again, Vader had been robbed.

Darth Vader had wanted to resume his pursuit of Luke Skywalker, but the Emperor had other plans in mind for his apprentice. After Vader had been directed to oversee the completion of a new superweapon, which had been under construction for some time in the Endor system, he had thought, The Emperor must know I tried to recruit my son to join me against him. He *knows* Luke could destroy him . . . and that I cannot do it alone.

And so the Emperor had done his best to keep Vader on a leash, instructing him to work with Prince Xizor, who controlled the galaxy's largest merchant fleet, which the Empire required to expedite shipping requirements to Endor. A Falleen, Xizor was also the head of the criminal organization known as Black Sun. Because Xizor had lost most of his family to Vader's genocidal actions on the Falleen homeworld, he had long desired vengeance, and schemed to discredit Vader and win favor with the Emperor. But when Vader learned that

Xizor had discovered his relationship to Luke Skywalker and had attempted to kill Luke, he ended his working arrangement with the Falleen most permanently by blasting Xizor and his personal skyhook — a large repulsor craft — out of Coruscant's upper atmosphere.

Construction on the Endor Project proceeded. A year after Vader's last encounter with Luke Skywalker, the Executor carried the Dark Lord to the still-unfinished superweapon.

Against Vader's objections, the Emperor — following a plan that had been conceived by Xizor — had allowed a computer that contained plans for the Endor Project to be transported on a single, unescorted freighter through the Both system. With the aid of Bothan spies, the Rebels had captured the computer to learn that the largest of Endor's nine moons was generating a powerful energy shield to protect the Empire's new "secret" battle station.

The Emperor was confident that the Rebels would take the bait and bring their fleet to Endor, but Vader was more interested in whatever future lay beyond that probable skirmish. Although he had proposed to the Emperor that Luke Skywalker could be converted to the dark side and join the Sith Lords, he was well aware of the Sith order's long tradition of limiting their number to two: one Master, one apprentice.

One of us will have to die, *Vader mused.*

CHAPTER TWENTY-ONE

The Endor Project was a new Death Star, which was suspended in a synchronous orbit around the forest-covered Sanctuary Moon of the gas giant Endor. When construction was completed, the new Death Star would be even larger than the original. Its primary weapon, the planet-destroying superlaser, had been redesigned so that it could be recharged within minutes and finely focused to fire at moving targets such as capital ships. Imperial technicians regarded it as the deadliest invention of all time.

As Vader's shuttle carried him from the *Executor* to the fragmentary framework of the new battle station, he surveyed the enormous superlaser with contempt. *Even if it succeeds where the first Death Star failed,* he thought, *it is an infant's trinket compared to the power of the Force.*

After landing, Vader informed the Death Star's commanding officer, Moff Jerjerrod, that the Emperor was displeased the station was not yet operational. Upon learning that the Emperor himself would soon be arriving in the Endor system, Jerjerrod commanded his men to redouble their efforts.

By the time the Emperor arrived via shuttle to a grand Imperial reception in a Death Star docking bay, Vader had received a report from Tatooine that Jabba the Hutt was dead. Evidently, Luke and his allies had successfully liberated Han Solo from the Hutt. After Vader informed the Emperor that the Death Star would be completed on schedule, the Emperor said, "You have done well, Lord Vader. And now I sense you wish to continue your search for young Skywalker."

"Yes, my Master."

"Patience, my friend," the Emperor rasped. "In time, he will seek you out. And when he does, you must bring him before *me*. He has grown *strong*. Only together can we turn him to the dark side of the Force."

"As you wish," said Vader. He had not forgotten how Anakin Skywalker had obeyed Palpatine's command to kill Count Dooku, and had no reason to doubt that the Emperor had already planned a test for Luke to determine whether Vader would remain his apprentice.

"Everything is proceeding as I have foreseen," the Emperor sneered.

As Vader escorted his Master through the Death Star, he wished he could see the future so clearly. Palpatine had lured Anakin Skywalker to the dark side, re-created him as a cybernetic monster, and remained the more powerful of the two Sith Lords. Although Luke Skywalker had defeated Vader at the first Death Star, evaded him on Hoth, and escaped him at Bespin, Vader did not believe his son could resist the Emperor's power.

Luke has to join me. I cannot lose again.

The new Death Star's construction continued. Vader had just learned that Rebel ships had assembled in the Sullust system when he was summoned to the Emperor's throne room. Perched atop a highly shielded tower at the station's north pole, the throne room had large circular windows that allowed the Emperor a wide view of the forest moon and the battle station's upper hemisphere. The throne itself was a high-backed seat that was set atop a broad, elevated platform. The back of the seat faced Vader as he mounted the steps that led to the throne.

"What is thy bidding, my Master?"

Swiveling in his throne to look at Vader, the Emperor said, "Send the fleet to the far side of Endor. There it will stay until called for."

"What of the reports of the Rebel fleet massing near Sullust?"

"It is of no concern," the Emperor said dismissively. "Soon the Rebellion will be crushed and young Skywalker will be one of us! Your work here is finished, my friend. Go to the command ship and await my orders."

Soon after Vader returned to the bridge of the *Executor*, he was looking through a viewport when he saw a *Lambda*-class shuttle approaching Endor. The shuttle had transmitted an older Imperial code for clearance, but Vader permitted the ship to proceed to the forest moon. *Luke is on that ship*, he sensed with utmost certainty.

Although the Emperor had instructed Vader to remain on the *Executor*, Vader was compelled to report this latest development in person. After returning to the Emperor's throne room on the Death Star, Vader noticed that the Emperor actually seemed surprised to hear that Luke had arrived on Endor.

"Are you sure?" the Emperor asked.

"I have *felt* him, my Master."

"Strange that I have not," the Emperor said warily. "I wonder if your feelings on this matter are clear, Lord Vader."

"They are clear, my Master."

"Then you must go to the Sanctuary Moon and wait for him."

Skeptical, Vader asked, "He will come to me?"

"I have foreseen it. His compassion for you will be his undoing. He will come to you, and then you will bring him before me."

"As you wish," Vader said. As he strode out of the throne room, he thought, *If the Emperor could not detect Luke's arrival, perhaps he has grown weak with age. If only I could take Luke far from here to persuade him to ally with me . . .*

For a moment, Vader allowed himself to imagine a future with his son. He imagined Luke as his apprentice — *I would teach him everything* — and as his partner — *he would keep me strong!* There would be no rivalry or secrets between them. With their bond of blood and shared power, they would be the greatest of Sith Lords.

We would be invincible. I will take him to Bast Castle and —

Vader remembered the vision that had come to him when he'd left Coruscant for Endor, the vision of his meeting with Luke at his fortress on Vjun. In that vision, Luke had joined him, and the Emperor had arrived with fire and death. Vader realized it didn't matter whether the vision had been a nightmare, premonition, psychic warning, or delusion, because it was a revelation of an event that could never transpire.

There is nowhere Luke and I could go. Nowhere we could hide.

Powerless to disobey his Master, Vader proceeded to his shuttle.

The largest Imperial structure on the Sanctuary Moon was the energy shield generator, a four-sided pyramidal tower that supported a wide focus dish that projected a deflector shield around the orbital Death

Star. Near this generator stood an elevated landing platform, which was illuminated by brilliant floodlights. A large area of natural forest had been cleared to accommodate both the generator and the platform, something that had not gone over well with the indigenous Ewok population.

A four-legged All Terrain Armored Transport walked along the edge of the forest and lurched toward the landing platform as Vader's shuttle touched down. After Vader disembarked, he went to a gantry to greet the AT-AT. The AT-AT's hatch slid up to reveal an Imperial Commander, three stormtroopers, and Luke Skywalker, whose wrists were secured by binders.

Luke had surrendered to the soldiers. He was dressed in a form-fitting black uniform, and Vader wondered if this might in any way suggest that Luke had already surrendered to the dark side as well. *No*, he thought. *Not yet*.

The soldiers presented Luke's lightsaber to Vader, who glanced at Luke's gloved right hand. *A new lightsaber*, he thought, *and a new hand. Just as in my vision of Bast Castle*.

After taking the proffered lightsaber, the Dark Lord said, "The Emperor has been expecting you."

"I know, Father."

Vader realized he actually enjoyed hearing Luke refer to him as *father*. Vader said, "So you have accepted the truth."

"I've accepted the truth that you were once Anakin Skywalker, my father."

Foolish boy. Facing Luke, Vader gave his son a hard stare through dark lenses as he said, "That name no longer has any meaning for me."

Luke tried to convince Vader that there was still good in him. He pleaded with his father to come with him, away from the forest moon and the Emperor.

"You don't know the power of the dark side," Vader said. "I must obey my Master."

"I will not turn," Luke vowed, "and you'll be forced to kill me."

I've done worse things, Vader thought. He said, "If that is your destiny —"

"Search your feelings, Father," Luke interrupted. "You can't do this. I feel the conflict within you. Let go of your hate."

If only I could, Vader thought. *If only I could.* He said, "It is too late for me, Son." Summoning two stormtroopers to lead Luke to the waiting shuttle, he added, "The Emperor will show you the true nature of the Force. He is your Master now."

Wearing an expression of sad resolve, Luke said, "Then my father is truly dead."

As Luke was escorted to the shuttle, Vader thought, *I must obey my Master. Even if it means the death of my son.*

And even it if means the death of me.

CHAPTER TWENTY-TWO

Vader delivered Luke to the tower atop the Death Star, where the Emperor — without rising from his throne — used the Force to release Luke from his binders. After Palpatine ordered his red-armored Royal Guards to leave the throne room, Vader presented Luke's new lightsaber for inspection. The Emperor was confident that Luke would join him as his father had.

Unimpressed by the Emperor, Luke refused to be converted to the dark side. However, his confidence was badly shaken when the Emperor confessed that it was he who had allowed the Rebel Alliance to learn the location of the Death Star and its shield generator, and that the Empire was completely prepared to deal with the imminent attack from the Rebel fleet.

As Luke looked through the throne room's tall windows to see the arrival of the Rebel ships, Vader sensed his son's increased anxiety. The space battle progressed, and it was obvious that the Rebel ships were greatly outnumbered by Imperial fighters. While the Emperor remained seated upon his throne, he taunted Luke, urging him to take back his lightsaber and give in to his anger. Again, Luke refused.

But then the Emperor revealed that the Death Star's superlaser was operational, and issued a command for the gunners to fire at will. An intense beam shot out from the Death Star toward a large Rebel cruiser, which exploded in a blinding flash.

The Emperor continued to goad Luke into retrieving his lightsaber. "Strike me down with all of your *hatred*," the Emperor spat, "and your journey to the dark side will be complete."

Using the Force, Luke snatched up his weapon, activated its blade, and swung fast at the Emperor's head. But Vader moved faster, activating his own lightsaber to deftly block Luke's attack. The sight of Vader and Luke crossing lightsabers excited and amused the Emperor, and he cackled with perverse glee. Vader recalled that Palpatine had laughed the same way over two decades ago, when he had ordered Anakin Skywalker to kill Count Dooku.

I was the victor then, Vader thought as he used his lightsaber to drive Luke away from the Emperor. *And the Force is with me now!*

As their duel carried on throughout the throne room, the Dark Lord sensed that Luke was drawing from his own anger to fuel his attack. From his throne, the Emperor said, "Good. Use your aggressive feelings, boy! Let the hate flow through you."

My Master wants *Luke to win*, Vader realized with some resentment. *I will not give him that satisfaction. I will not be —*

Unexpectedly, Luke deactivated his lightsaber and said, "I will not fight you, Father."

"You are unwise to lower your defenses," Vader said, as he brought his lightsaber up fast. With incredible speed, Luke reactivated his weapon to parry Vader's attack. Vader swung again and again, but Luke blocked each blow. Soon, Vader was breathing hard through his respirator. *I can't let Luke defeat me*, Vader thought. *I won't let the Emperor have him!*

A precise kick from Luke sent Vader over the edge of the elevated platform. Crashing upon the metal floor below, Vader roared as he felt a cybernetic cable snap in his right leg. Luke tried to distance himself from Vader by leaping to a catwalk that stretched across the throne room's ceiling. "Your thoughts betray you, Father," Luke said. "I feel the good in you . . . the conflict."

Rising from the floor below with obvious discomfort, Vader said, "There is no conflict."

"You couldn't bring yourself to kill me before," Luke said as he moved across the catwalk, "and I don't believe you'll destroy me now."

Shifting his focus to the metal supports that secured the catwalk to the ceiling, Vader said, "If you will not fight, then you will meet your destiny."

The Dark Lord flung his still-activated lightsaber upward. Luke ducked the red blade, but was unable to stop it from cutting through the catwalk's supports, which tore from the ceiling and sent Luke tumbling to the floor below. Vader watched Luke roll out of view under the Emperor's elevated platform.

Vader's lightsaber had deactivated and landed on the floor several meters away from him. He extended his hand as the lightsaber flew up from the floor to return to his grip. He activated the weapon's blade and walked down a flight of steps to the area below the platform, where metal girders offered numerous hiding places. Outside the Death Star and on the Sanctuary Moon, the Empire's battle with the Rebels raged on, but Vader could not care less. As far as he was concerned, his duel with Luke was the *only* battle that mattered.

Searching the shadows below the platform for the slightest movement, the father said, "You cannot hide forever, Luke."

From the darkness, the son said, "I will not fight you."

"Give yourself to the dark side," Vader urged. "It is the only way you can save your friends." Vader was suddenly aware that Luke was now thinking of his friends, his concern for them almost palpable. "Yes,"

Vader said, "your thoughts betray you. Your feelings for them are strong. Especially for . . ."

Luke was unable to stop Vader from accessing his mind.

"Sister!" Vader exclaimed. "So . . . you have a twin sister. Your feelings have now betrayed her too. Obi-Wan was wise to hide her from me. Now his failure is complete." Moving deeper into the recesses below the platform, he said, "If you will not turn to the dark side, then perhaps she will."

"No!" Luke screamed, igniting his lightsaber as he rushed from his hiding place to attack Vader. Sparks flew as they traded blows in the dark, cramped area, and Vader was forced to retreat out from under the platform until they arrived at the edge of a short bridge beside a deep, open elevator shaft.

A glancing blow ruptured Vader's life-support system, and as he fell back against the bridge's railing he was unable to stop Luke's blade from severing his right wrist. Metal and electronic parts flew from Vader's shattered stump, and his lightsaber clattered over the edge of the bridge and into the apparently bottomless shaft. Badly wounded and utterly exhausted, Vader looked up to see Luke's lightsaber angled to deliver a killing stroke.

The Emperor had risen from his throne to stand on the stairway behind Luke. "Good!" the Emperor said. "Your hate has made you powerful. Now, fulfill your destiny and take your father's place at *my* side!"

So this is how it all ends, Vader thought.

But then Luke deactivated his lightsaber and said, "Never!" Flinging the weapon aside, he declared, "I'll never turn to the dark side. You've failed, Your Highness. I am a Jedi, like my father before me."

The Emperor scowled. With immeasurable displeasure, he said, "So be it . . . *Jedi.* If you will not be turned, you will be *destroyed.*"

Still lying against the bridge railing beside the elevator shaft, Vader watched the Emperor extend his gnarled fingers and unleash blinding bolts of blue lightning from his fingertips. The lightning struck Luke, who tried to deflect the crackling bands of energy, but was so overwhelmed that his body crumpled to the floor.

No, Vader thought. *No. Not like this.*

As the Emperor continued to strike Luke with his barrage of Sith lightning, Vader struggled to his feet. One leg was broken, and the other wasn't working right. Moving awkwardly, he shifted his bulk to stand beside his Master. On the floor, Luke writhed in agony, and was on the verge of death as he groaned, "Father, please. Help me."

Vader watched Luke curl into a fetal position as the Emperor hurled an even more staggering wave of lightning at his victim. Vader had no doubt that Luke was about to die. His son screamed.

Not just my son . . .

The Emperor unleashed another round of lightning.

. . . or Padmé's son . . .

Luke screamed louder.

. . . but my son . . . who loves me.

Luke's clothes began to smolder as his body involuntarily spasmed. Suddenly, Vader realized that he was no longer concerned about his own personal future. Despite all the terrible, unspeakable things he'd done in his life, he knew he could not stand by and allow the Emperor to kill Luke. And in that moment of awareness, he was Darth Vader no more.

He was Anakin Skywalker.

It took all of his remaining strength to seize the Emperor from behind, lift him off his feet, and carry him to the open elevator shaft. The wretched Emperor continued to release lightning bolts, but they veered away from Luke and arced back to crash down upon him and his insurgent apprentice. The lightning penetrated Vader's life-support suit and electrified Anakin's organic remains, but he lurched forward until he could throw the Emperor into the elevator shaft.

Palpatine screamed as his body plummeted down the shaft. Still trapped within Darth Vader's armor, Anakin collapsed at the shaft's edge, but heard the explosion of dark energy that consumed the falling Emperor.

Hearing his own breathing as a rasping rattle, Anakin knew that Vader's helmet's respiratory apparatus was broken. He felt something tug at his shoulders, and realized Luke had crawled beside him and was pulling him away from the edge of the abyss.

Despite his own injuries, Luke managed to haul his father to the hangar that contained Vader's shuttle. The journey was made even more difficult by the fact that the Rebels had disabled the energy shield projector on the Sanctuary Moon, and the Death Star was now under heavy attack. Trying to keep his own legs steady as the battle station was wracked by explosions, Luke dragged his father to the shuttle's landing ramp before he collapsed from the effort.

He's not going to make it, Anakin thought. *Not with me.*

"Luke," he gasped, "help me take this mask off."

Luke knelt beside him and said, "But you'll die."

"Nothing can stop that now," Anakin said. "Just for once . . . let me look on you . . . with my own eyes."

Slowly, carefully, Luke lifted Vader's angular helmet, then removed the faceplate from the black durasteel shell that wrapped around his neck. As Anakin's scarred features were exposed, he was surprised to feel tears welling in his eyes.

It's over, he thought. *The nightmare is over.*

He smiled weakly, then said, "Now . . . go, my son. Leave me."

"No," Luke insisted. "You're coming with me. I'll not leave you here. I've got to save you."

Anakin smiled again. "You already have, Luke. You were right." Choking his last breaths, he said, "You were right about me. Tell your sister . . . you were right."

Closing his eyes as he slumped back against the shuttle ramp, Anakin Skywalker had every reason to believe that he was finally about to embrace perpetual darkness.

Not for the first time, he was wrong.

EPILOGUE

Initially, there *was* darkness for Anakin Skywalker, a boundless shadowy realm, like a universe without stars. But then, from somewhere at the edge of his awareness, he perceived a distant, shimmering light, then heard a voice say, *Anakin.*

The voice was familiar.

Although Anakin no longer had a body or a mouth with which to speak, he somehow answered, *Obi-Wan? Master, I'm so sorry. So very, very —*

Anakin, listen carefully, Obi-Wan interrupted, and Anakin was aware that the distant light was either growing brighter or closer, or perhaps both. *You are in the netherworld of the Force, but if you ever wish to revisit corporeal space, then I still have one thing left to teach you. A way to become one with the Force. If you choose this path to immortality, then you must listen now, before your consciousness fades.*

Knowing he was beyond redemption, Anakin said, *But, Master . . . why me?*

Because you ended the horror, Anakin, Obi-Wan said. *Because you fulfilled the prophecy.*

The light was very bright now.

Anakin's first thought was that he might be able to see his children again. He said, *Thank you, Master.*

Taking the Imperial shuttle, Luke Skywalker had escaped with his father's remains from the Death Star only a moment before the battle station exploded. After landing on the Sanctuary Moon, Luke prepared a very private funeral in a forest clearing.

Night had fallen by the time Luke placed Anakin Skywalker's armor-clad body atop a pile of gathered wood. As he ignited the pyre, Luke said, "I burn his armor and with it the name of Darth Vader. May the name of Anakin Skywalker be a light that guides the Jedi for generations to come."

Luke was unaware of the spirits who watched him from the shadows of the lambent woods. But later, when he rejoined his allies for their victory celebration in the treetop village that was home to the Ewoks, Luke saw three shimmering apparitions materialize in the darkness. They were Obi-Wan Kenobi, Yoda . . . and his father, Anakin Skywalker.

The Jedi had returned.

ABOUT THE AUTHOR

Ryder Windham has written many *Star Wars* books, including junior novelizations of the *Star Wars* trilogy (Scholastic), *Revenge of the Sith Scrapbook* (Random House), and *Star Wars: The Ultimate Visual Guide* (DK). He is also the author of the nonfiction books *What You Don't Know About Animals*, *What You Don't Know About Mysterious Places*, and *What You Don't Know About Dangerous Places* (Scholastic). He lives with his family in Providence, Rhode Island.